Sometimes life may feel, like, too complicated...

... but there's always a way through the maze when we try to help others.

FROM THE SAME AUTHOR
In this series:
Flip! On the Edge
Flip! Beyond the Horizon
Flip! The Daisychain

In the White Gates series:
The Kicking Tree
Ultimate Justice
Winds & Wonders
The Spark

The third book in the Flip trilogy

FLIP!

THE DAISY CHAIN

EVIL RELIES ON LIES BUT GOODNESS DELIGHTS IN THE
TRUTH WHICH NEVER GOES AWAY

TREVOR STUBBS

THE
LISTENING
PEOPLE

The Listening People
15 Cleeve Grove
Keynsham,
Bristol, BS31 2HF

Email: author@trevorstubbs.co.uk
Web: www.trevorstubbs.co.uk

ISBN 978-0-9550100-5-7

British Library Cataloguing in Publication Data.
A catalogue record for this book is available from the British Library.

THE
LISTENING
PEOPLE

For the amazing students and staff at Bishop Gwynne College in Juba, South Sudan, who achieve so much with so little.

We call upon you, brothers and sisters. Encourage people who are low in self-confidence. Warn those who are lazy, care for the weak and be patient with each and every person.

Let no one repay evil with evil but continually do good to each other and to everybody.

Rejoice always, no matter what.

St Paul's first letter to the Thessalonians, 50 CE.

1

The shock was intense. Alice wept; the pain was unexpected and excruciating. "What the...!"? she yelled.

The five - who had only moments before been so determined to stick together no matter what - were letting go of each other not knowing what to do.

Alice made out Tom's calming voice despite the pain in her bare legs. "Just stingers! Nasty ones. But they won't kill us."

Nadia, who was not usually lost for words, sought among her vocabulary for something that would express her pain and shock. She failed and simply uttered, "Sugar!"

Roxanne laughed. "That's all you got to say, Nadia?"

"Get me outa here," she retorted. "I - hate - skirts!"

Blessed with voluminous thick trousers, Hen took charge. "Stay where you are. Don't move. Tom and I will get you out."

The boys waded in and lifted Nadia and Roxanne clear of the offending plants.

Tom returned for Alice and back on safe turf, he lowered her gently onto the sward like a medieval gallant and looked around for some dock leaves. It didn't take him long and - taking the role of a nurse - helped Alice rub the juice into her legs.

"You all OK?" asked Hen. "I mean apart from the nettles?"

Despite re-entering in the middle of a patch of vicious stinging nettles beside a Scottish drystone wall, the five sixteen-year-olds were otherwise unharmed.

However, somewhere in the process Nadia had managed to step into something else. "Effing dog muck!" she swore.

"No," corrected Hen. "Not dog. It's sheep droppings."

"Same difference," protested Nadia.

"Not quite," began Hen. He looked about to explain the niceties but, seeing Nadia's expression decided otherwise.

"Do you think this is the same place as the Nazi world but in ours?" asked Tom. They had crossed a ridge in the fifth but it had been smooth and rounded, not angular like the one they had encountered the first time.

Hen took in the scene. There was no one in any direction as far as the eye could see. He was thinking.

"As we set off, I did see a broken wall," ventured Roxanne, "but we were heading for a gap in it. I reckon we have managed to cross over into some other world in which the wall hasn't fallen down."

"I agree," said Hen. "We've definitely crossed over into a new parallel – the vortex was back on the left. But if it's our world or not we can't tell."

Alice went cold and then hot all over. If this was yet another parallel world, were they doomed to keep moving on, never getting home? The combination of dread and doubt made what she said sound bitter.

"Yes. I know my left from my right!" She didn't look up but engrossed herself in rubbing her stings with a dock leaf. "And I can't stand skirts! Especially on a mountain top," she added, morosely.

Tom knew where this was coming from. "On the plus side we're together," he ventured, softly.

"That just means there are *five* of us on a bleak nettle-ridden, poo-covered mountainside in a world that is probably still in the stone age," she whined.

Hen continued to take stock of what he saw. "I think that assessment might be a little hasty," he began, in analytical tones.

Alice became angry and dismissive. "How do you know that?"

"No falling out, remember!" said Tom, calmly.

"I... I wasn't ..." spluttered Alice, defensively.

"All for one and one for all... *whatever*," chanted Nadia, gingerly.

Roxanne wasn't saying anything. She remained quiet, sitting with her shoulder against Nadia's.

"Back to the situation in point," resumed Hen. "We can say for certain that we are no longer in the Nazi world; we are in a parallel world that maintains its walls. It's the same wall but in better condition; it has been erected to control sheep - Nadia has found the poo. And here..." Hen pulled some wool from between the stones in the wall, "is more evidence. See the blue dye? This means these farmers use indelible ink to brand their stock. Hardly stone age."

"A better world, then," muttered Alice, feeling a little more cheerful. "So could be our world?"

"It could," said Hen. "But we cannot assume it is - it could be a third place."

"If it's a third place, it could be the best world of all," mused Nadia. "No Nazis and no Padget."

"It could but it wouldn't be *ours*," sighed Alice, feeling cross again. She was fighting off waves of homesickness; she couldn't help it. But she wasn't going to mention her nice stable family in front of Nadia and Rox. "I mean, I think it is our job to remain in *our* world and try and make it better. I'm glad we won the Second World War. A lot of people died - millions - trying to defeat the Nazis. I am really going to do my little bit toward avoiding doing all of those things again."

"You - us - and who's army?" murmured Nadia.

"I can think of lots of people," answered, Alice. But, put to

4

it, she couldn't think of anyone who would risk much. She could even hear her mother telling her to keep her head down and stay out of things that were too big for her.

"We can keep telling people what we believe," said Tom. "Help people to recognise the dangers."

Roxanne tuned in. "When I was at home, I never thought I could do anything but my time with the MPC has taught me that you can't keep the truth from being spoken. Just a few people can make all the difference. All oppressors fall in the end. There was this guy who just took a placard out into Trafalgar Square that said: 'Hitler can't stop me being free.' He climbed on to one of them lions and it took several minutes to get him down. There were two others with him who filmed him being pulled down and dragged away. Loads of people have seen that footage. He's a hero."

"What happened to him?" asked Nadia.

"It was brilliant. The Sestapo decided they would make an example of him and they executed him, publicly."

"Brilliant?!" exclaimed Alice. "How could that be brilliant?"

"It made people realise they had to do something to stop the BUF. Loads of young people joined the resistance. Instead of making people weaker, it made them stronger. The truth is stronger than lies."

"And love is stronger than hate," added Hen. "We can

make a huge difference in our world by outing Donald Padget and his cronies. Up to now, we've been trying to avoid getting used and rescuing Nadia. We've done that – and found Rox. At the moment, Padget's no idea where we are, so now is the time to expose him... *if* we are in our world."

"So we need to get off this hillside and find out," stated Tom.

"Then, if it *is* our world, find a phone and ring our people and the police," concluded Alice.

"Forward," yelled Tom, giving Alice a high five. "How about we go back to the house we left? Those people could still be there, only, this time they'll be on our side."

"An interesting thought," mused Hen. "But I think I would like to go on to meet someone new."

"Yeah. Turning up in their clothes would be kind of spooky," smiled Nadia.

"I'm with Hen. I vote we go down into the next valley," elected Roxanne.

As they set off, they chatted about the wonderful scenery and how they were going to stay friends, no matter what, for the rest of their lives - all the while wondering what parallel world they had entered..

They cleared a hilltop to see a wide valley open before them. There were a few farmhouses up the top end and, as it curved away from them, the glen opened out and a cluster of houses hinted at the beginning of a village or perhaps a town.

A thought occurred to Hen. "I don't want to alarm you guys," he said. "We don't know exactly where we are and, more specifically, how far we are from Donald Padget's Inverlochie estate. The last thing we want to do is to walk right back into his hands. But the Scottish Highlands is a pretty extensive place, and we haven't seen a castle or a loch so we should be OK. Always assuming this *is* our world..."

"Better be," muttered Alice, under her breath.

Nadia shrugged. She wasn't worried. "Donald Padget won't be here, though - in Scotland. He was in London... and he might even have gone back to America."

"And he has no reason to visit his estate," said Hen. "But it would be wise to keep clear of it, anyway."

2

The sun began to beat down as the four youngsters reached a wooded slope. The trees came to an end, however, and they crossed a field and followed a footpath along the banks of a river. They were pretty thirsty; they must find a habitation soon. Rounding a bend, they found themselves in a flat green field and were making their happy way across it toward a stone bridge when they heard the sound of a motor. A quad bike mounted the bridge and crossed it. They waved but it drove on into a field beyond.

Had they followed him, they would have seen the rider check his mobile for a signal. There were tourists on his land again – this time a mad bunch of teenagers dressed like some kind of modern-day hippies – crossing his lower pasture without proper care. He was angry. The American laird was a menace – all sorts of people from the castle came and went as if he and his animals and crops weren't there. The farmer was sure this gang must be the latest to come from the castle, so he phoned the estate office to get their "bloody teenagers" off his land immediately.

The farmer used to respect the former laird – the whole community did – but this new foreigner earned their contempt.

The phone was answered by Audra McBlair

"Your American laird might be the land-owner but he doesn't work this farm," he complained. "Proper landowners should be sensitive to the needs of those who manage the land and whose livelihoods depend on it."

McBlair apologised sweetly and said they would get someone out to his place straight away. She was sitting in her office at Inverlochie Castle flanked by a stern-looking Donald Padget and a defeated Professor Williams.

McBlair called her driver and ordered him to take the van with a couple of men and pick up the offending kids.

"It's amazing," she said, annoyed. "You're looking for missing teenagers and then you end up having to look after someone else's...! I'll be glad when I no longer have to keep the locals sweet... Where are *your* kids then, professor?"

Professor Williams shrugged. He genuinely had no idea.

"I'll find them, Commander." Padget spoke more reassuringly than he felt. "They'll come to light soon enough. If the youngsters decided to hitch-hike, the traffic on the Finchley Road would have taken them north. I have posted my sleuths on the major routes at the service stations on the M1, A1 and M40. So far, we have had no sightings and we've also been keeping a discreet watch on the home in Leeds of one of the girls. She hasn't turned up there but I have been informed that her parents have been followed to Leeds City station where they boarded a train for King's Cross. That might be significant; they were clearly not expecting their daughter. So my guess is she's still somewhere in the London area... It's just a matter of time," he reiterated, with false confidence. "Four human beings can't just disappear, can they?"

Prof W knew differently but he said nothing.

Padget's smartphone – the latest model, costing a fortune – bleeped. It was a text from Wood. He was on his way from Prestwick. Padget had summoned him to Inverlochie – he needed him by his side. Before he left, Wood had reported that the police were onto the five's disappearance. It had been due to some interfering youth club leader. This was not good news.

3

When the estate van arrived in the lane to the farm, the driver pulled up and offered to help the youngsters. He leaned out of his cab and volunteered to take them to the village but there was no way any of them were getting into an enclosed van again – albeit this one was red and new-looking.

Nadia said a few choice words about vans. Alice apologised and said they had had a bad experience of vans; they'd prefer to walk. Hen spoke up in his polite tones and asked directions, promising to keep to the road when he heard of the farmer's complaints.

"Did you see the daisy on his cap?" said Nadia, after the van had gone.

"Yeah," said Hen. "I did. Just like the one on the Inverlochie website."

"Oh, no," sighed Alice. "It can't be!"

"What kind of man wears a cap with a daisy on it?" asked Roxanne.

"A dangerous one," said Tom. "I would venture to suggest we're certainly back in our world and dangerously near the Inverlochie estate."

The daisy people! Alice shuddered. *My family are in this world – but at this moment when we really need them I have no chance of contacting them; they might as well be on another planet.* "As soon as we get to those woods up ahead," she suggested, "we should get off this track and run!"

The van driver phoned in to say that the five teenagers reported by the tenant farmer had been located – three girls and two lads – but they had declined to get into the van; they had promised to keep to the road. McBlair asked how old they were.

"About sixteen. They're a right bunch... very oddly dressed in old-fashioned clothes too big for them. Never seen nothing like it. One lad's got a posh accent. There're three girls – one with brown hair, a blonde that sounds northern English and a black girl who has a distinct dislike of vans and doesn't mind saying so. Oh, and a big lad that didn't say anything."

"That makes five," counted McBlair.

The driver confirmed.

McBlair relayed the description

"If there were four, not five, I might think they were ours," shrugged Padget. "Can't imagine what they would be doing here, though."

Professor Williams stiffened.

"You seem surprised, Williams. Do you think these are our

gang?" Padget stared the professor in the eye.

"I... I... maybe," he stammered. "There are a lot of—"

Commander McBlair looked into the professor's eyes with a searing gaze. "But you know something, don't you Professor? Five. I think you know who this extra girl might be. Am I right?"

Prof W nodded. He stammered. "If it's... it's them it could be Roxanne Battie. She was also at the clinic at one time."

Padget sneered. His confidence and authority were rushing back. This was a remarkable stroke of luck. "Ah, yes. Was she the one you 'lost' last year? You seem to make a habit of losing your subjects, Williams."

Prof W lowered his head.

Padget smirked. "Well, it may be the quarry has walked straight into the bears' lair ... do you see yourself as a bear, Williams? No, perhaps not; more of a weasel with a den in which you dissect your prey. Nasty piece of stuff, aren't you? I can just imagine what the courts would do to you if they were to catch you." Prof W understood the threat and said nothing.

McBlair called the van driver and ordered him to pick up the five whether they liked it or not.

The van intercepted them before they could escape into the woods and the driver ordered them to get in. Hen began to protest but two beefy men jumped out of the back. The friends began to run but this time it was their assailants who had the advantage of surprise.

The men caught up with Nadia whose voluminous attire was difficult to run in. They grabbed her, lifting her off her feet and, despite the assaults of the others, carried her towards the open rear doors of the van. Tom pulled one of the men off her and found himself a match for him. He had never been a fighter but he was strong. Alice decided she would have a go at biting one of the men's naked arms. It had the desired effect and he let go of Nadia, who kicked out and caught the third a hefty blow with her foot. Hen ordered Nadia to run which she did and then he set about the second man who had turned on Alice.

Nadia scaled a gate which led into a field and Alice followed her. Roxanne picked up a rock and hit Tom's man between the shoulders and floored him. Tom and Roxanne ran towards Hen who slipped from his man's grasp. All three dodged further attempts to grab them and they cleared the gate too – Tom with a gate vault that caused his foot to connect with his pursuer's jaw – and then all five were heading across the field for their lives.

The men were in no condition to run after them. One was still trying to work out whether he had a broken back – he hadn't. The second cradled his jaw while the driver was attending to Alice's nasty bite.

The five friends were trying to find a way out of the field and had just decided they would have to climb a drystone wall when there was a loud report from a shotgun and shot whizzed over their heads. They crouched down in front of the wall as another blast sent shot ricocheting off the top-most stones. The farmer paused to reload.

"Sorry, guys," grunted Hen. "Nice try but I reckon the game is up."

"No it ain't," protested Nadia. "There's no way that farmer is aiming to hit us. He'll be up before the beak and thrown in jug and he don't want that. He's just trying to scare us."

"Logical," said Hen but Nadia had already begun climbing the wall and Hen thought he should follow. He hadn't got to the top, however, before Nadia jumped back down with a start. She had seen what the field beyond the wall contained: a large black bull with wild-looking eyes. He had been spooked by the noise in the midst of a peaceful cud-chewing session and was not happy. Nadia and bulls did not mix!

They were trapped. In front of them, the three men from the van were over the gate and closing in, the irate farmer was brandishing his shiny shotgun from the road and a mad bull cut off their retreat behind.

Hen stood with his hands up.

"Out of the ruddy frying-pan and into the effing fire,"

uttered Nadia.

The men rounded up their quarry carefully, leaving no opportunity for another fight. They bundled them into the van as the farmer stood with his gun at the ready.

4

Donald Padget greeted the young people with a huge grin upon his face. He was flanked by a woman wearing a badge that announced her as Audra McBlair. She also wore a small daisy broach.

"Well, hello!" Padget taunted them. "So *you* have come to find *me* - or perhaps your professor who is so keen to complete his investigations...? Oh, don't look like that! You will be doing something to advance not only science but also the world. Oh, yes. With your help, we can deal a final blow to the wishy-washy inefficiencies of the Western world - perhaps even the whole world in due course... What? Nothing to say for yourselves?"

"Heard 'em telling each other to keep mum," volunteered the driver.

Padget mocked them. "Oh, dear. That will never do. How long do you think you can keep that up?"

"Just threaten this one, boss," laughed the driver, grabbing Nadia by the arm, "and I warrant they'll bleat like sheep."

"Is that so? I'll bear that in mind... Now, should I take a picture of you so that when the time comes, I can post it on

Instagram or Snapchat, or whatever you young people use these days? You see I'm up with all the silly social media...You do look a sight," he teased. "No. Sadly, I cannot post anything just yet but I *will* take a picture – you are sooo wonderfully dressed..." He took out his state-of-the-art mobile. "Smile. Oh, come on, such cheerless faces."

The driver released his hold of Nadia to avoid being in the picture. Nadia did not need a second invitation. She took two brisk steps forward, grabbed Padget's phone out of his hand and threw it as hard as she could on the floor at her feet. The effect was impressive. The glass smashed instantly and the rest of the slim, but significantly meaty device, bounced a few centimetres before Nadia crunched it under her shoe with all her weight and then kicked it, hard. It ricocheted off the wall and eventually came to rest by Padget's boot. Instinctively, Alice gave Nadia a look of triumph and raised her hand in a high five which Nadia met.

Padget's change of colour was amazing. He was so shocked it took him a few seconds to take in what had happened, long enough for Prof W to intervene and prevent an untimely murder.

"Don't damage the goods," he said, faintly.

Padget brought himself under control and his complexion regained some of its former cast. "Feisty, eh? Your professor has chosen well for you to be the first subject for his dissections... Get them out of here!" he barked. "And I want them cleaned up and clothed in something like normal for their age. Amusing though it is, we don't want to beg attention."

Up to the moment Nadia had smashed Padget's phone, Alice had been feeling a mixture of anger and defeat. Why had it been so easy for Padget? Of all places to re-emerge on their side! The fates, or whatever, had it in for them. She hadn't done anything to deserve this; she hadn't asked to be given the ability to flip. Perhaps if she'd split – carried on running when they'd grabbed Nadia – she might have got away and got herself home. She was fast – they wouldn't have caught her. But instead she had stopped with the others. Had that been a mistake? But when Nadia took on Padget like that – in an act of pure defiance – she was proud of her. *No*, she told herself in that moment, *Alice Downey, you made the right decision. What you did was right.* She felt inches taller as she was bundled off by some attendant sporting a daisy on the cord of her heavy spectacles.

When they had gone, Padget swept aside the bits of phone with his foot and said calmly, "Thank you Commander. You see the value of this exercise?..." Then he turned to the driver. "We will leave when Wood gets here... Williams – you're coming, too."

"But–"

"Do you *want* me to throw you to the wolves, Williams?"

"No... I–"

"Abducting children – then their murder... I think we can make it look rather horrible. They'll send you down for life. Which might not be a long one in prison; other prisoners do some quite disgusting things to child killers, I'm told."

"You... you're despicable!" blurted the professor.

"Me?" sneered Padget, "No, professor. It is *you* who proposed preparing one of them in perfectly good health for a postmortem. She seems to be just the ticket... One hour."

☆☆☆

The young people were led to the bathrooms and forced to strip off their recently acquired ill-fitting Highland country garb at gunpoint. The three girls were ushered into a bathroom and, finally, left to wash themselves. Alice was wondering whether they would have to shower under the leering gaze of the attendant but she slammed the door.

Roxanne put out her tongue. Alice shuddered.

"They ain't gonna do nothing to us," said Nadia. "They daren't touch us – mustn't mess with the goods."

They turned on the shower and Alice relaxed.

"Hey, guys," called Nadia, through the streaming water. "You lot could've just let them take me back there; you could've split. It took two of the thugs to get me and there were only three of them. They'd have never caught you, Alice. Like, you could've been out of the county before they got started. You could have legged it and gone home... gone to the police or somut. You could have saved yourself but you didn't... You didn't desert me."

"I can't say I didn't think about it," admitted Alice.

"Course you did. Bound to have done. But you didn't. That's what matters." Nadia gave Alice a huge smile.

"It's, like, we're bound together," explained Alice. "I couldn't have run away leaving you with them."

Roxanne slid a hand down her arm with the fading scars. "There just ain't no way I'm going to leave any one of you. It's not until you've got people – real friends – that you realise just how important that is. It's, like, we're fam. There's no way I could have left you to these thugs."

"That's it," affirmed Alice. "That's the difference between us and them: heart."

"Exactly!" exclaimed Roxanne. "There's no heart in fascism. No love. No giving of yourself to help others. That's how you know them... And, in the end, they'll destroy themselves. They want things to be tidy, ordered and arranged in a way that puts them in control. Anything or anyone that doesn't fit they will try to sweep away without a second thought."

"But you can't put people into tidy boxes - they're, just, all different," stated Alice.

"Yeah. And no one is more important than anyone else," added Nadia.

"Exactly," smiled Roxanne.

5

Five clean and brushed teenagers – now dressed in contemporary but boring clothes – were bundled roughly into the back of the red van once more.

"Just one thing before you go," smiled McBlair. She mounted the step. "Let us make you more comfortable. Your arms, please." She produced a set of five syringes. "No need to look like that! This is nothing to worry about. It's just a sedative – you know the professor is most insistent that you are not damaged."

They were in no position to fight. Wood, the driver, and the two other beefy gentlemen were standing by and Padget and Prof W were within earshot.

"Get lost!" blurted Nadia. "I don't do drugs."

"If I don't have your arms, I shall jab your buttocks," snapped the commander.

Hen bared his arm. "Don't expect me to smile. That would be unreasonable. What you are doing is quite reprehensible."

"So you have a voice after all!" said McBlair. "No, nothing reprehensible. What we are doing is saving the world from itself. Unlike other attempts, our movement will not reveal itself until we have all the weapons at our disposal. And your 5D is going to be one of them. You will be contributing to the salvation of humanity – a human society in which all weaknesses will be eliminated and namby-pamby states replaced with crisp, clean pure administrations. Words of weakness like 'empathy', 'alternative', 'God' and 'religion' will be expunged from the dictionary. If the professor doesn't need you all for his experiments, you may prove valuable soldiers when you understand the rightness of our cause. You have much potential young man. I suggest you don't spoil yourself by selling your soul to live among riffraff."

"Oh I see," said Hen with the kind of voice he used when being a double agent. "That does make some kind of sense. And by riffraff you mean my friends here whom you are going to experiment on?"

"Well, I think one or two of them can be spared, don't you? I'm sure you, however, will prove an ally and asset to the cause; you have the breeding. But at the moment you cannot be trusted – if you prove yourself, your time will come. So, for now, this will help." McBlair plunged the needle into Hen's arm. "Next."

"If you think I'm going to let you stick that thing in me," yelled Nadia, "you've another think– Ow. Effing hell!" she gasped as McBlair pierced her upper thigh through her jeans.

"I warned you. Next."

Alice, Roxanne and Tom saw there was no point in fighting this. They took their lead from Hen.

The van drove off and they could talk in the back without being heard. "Just in case you're wondering," said Hen – their captors out of earshot. "There is no way I will ever be convinced of the virtues of a fascist state. We've seen first hand what that looks like. I passionately believe every unique human being is of infinite worth. Now, having been to the Nazi flipside, I am *utterly* convinced. We are all children of God, no matter who we are."

"You've got it all sorted – the words, I mean," said Alice, "I wish I was as sure of things."

"But you *are*, Alice. You know what's right and what's wrong, good or bad," Hen insisted.

"I'm not so good at putting it into words, though."

"But you believe in caring and looking after other people."

"Oh, yes. Of course," confirmed Alice.

"Then your actions will speak as loud as your words – louder even. That high five with Nadia back there said it all."

"Thanks," grinned Alice. "I meant that. Nadia, what you did there with Padget's phone was brilliant."

"Couldn't stand him standing there all la-di-da thinking he'd got his way," shrugged Nadia. "Didn't think much – I just did it... Worked, though, didn't it? He almost lost it, didn't he?"

They became silent; the drugs were definitely working. The van stopped at a junction and they could hear the clicking of the indicators.

"Where you taking us?" demanded Nadia.

Wood leaned back over his seat in the front. "Shut it! Or I'll get the commander to jab you again!"

They turned left and then they were speeding down a major road.

Nadia shouted as loudly as she could, "You ain't getting my brain. If I can't get away, I'll blow my own head off."

"Shut it!" shouted Wood again from the front.

"Or what?" demanded Nadia, "You going to blast me with that shotgun of yours? If you do, that daddy-boy back there will blast you. Don't forget, I'm precious cargo – not to be damaged." Wood ignored her and the van sped up.

"Are any of you feeling sleepy?" said Tom, quietly.

"Yes," said Hen. "It's the sedative; it's kicking in."

Feeling this was her last chance before the drugs took effect, Nadia lunged at the front seats and yelled, "Shoot me then, before I get past caring." But she fell short. Tom pulled her back and then she slowed down and almost passed out.

When they were all silent and still, Wood grunted, "About bloody time. When I signed up for this, I didn't reckon on managing ruddy teenagers. If you ask me, every one of them over thirteen should be taken off the streets and locked up until they're twenty-one."

By the time the red van had pulled into the port of Ullapool, the young people were barely conscious. Transferring them to a fishing boat was not going to be an easy matter under the eyes of the large number of tourists and locals that thronged the harbour. Wood was keen to avoid attention. Loading them bound and gagged would be impossible. His idea was that they would look like disabled children being taken for a ride.

They began by handing Hen from man to man down the gangplank onto the deck and then down below. Nadia was next, and then Alice and Roxanne, followed by Tom.

6

Though his world was hazy, Tom was aware of this being a fishing boat; the smell of the sea and the fish, and the call of the herring gulls resonated within him. Could he be home? No. This quayside was not home. This was a different port. After they were safely stowed in a smelly hold, Tom tried hard to shrug off the influence of the drug but before he could move, out of the corner of his eye he saw Wood approach with a syringe and check on Hen. Hen was clearly far from with it and Wood did not inject him. Then he left Alice, Roxanne and Nadia who were all still unconscious. When it was his turn he played dead. There was no way he wanted another dose. Wood seemed satisfied.

The smelly hold was shut and everything was dark. Tom heard the hatch being fastened down. After a few more minutes the boat began to throb with the powering of the engines and he felt the thump of the small waves as they moved out into the open sea. Tom's eyes gradually became accustomed to the darkness and he sat up to see Hen already up a ladder surveying the hatch.

"Thought you were asleep," Tom said.

Hen put his finger to his lips and whispered. "Only pretending. Didn't want another shot."

"Me neither," said Tom.

"They gave the girls the same dose as us. Being lighter it will have affected them more," explained Hen. "I guess we're in the bilges of some ship."

"The hold of a wooden trawler. Not very big. Less than twenty feet, I guess. Been used as a scalloper." Tom produced a piece of scallop shell he had felt beneath him.

"I forgot you are a sailor."

"I would like to be. Not much money in fishing these days, though."

"So they augment their income by transporting human cargo," sighed Hen. "Where do you think they are taking us?"

"Could be anywhere in these waters. You don't usually take this kind of boat far beyond the sight of land, though," explained Tom, feeling a little more useful than of late.

"Not America then?"

"Not in this boat. Apart from the fact that she isn't big enough to weather a mid-Atlantic storm, there isn't enough storage for a lengthy voyage."

"Twenty feet – that's, what, seven metres?"

"Less," said Tom.

"So there won't be many up top?" suggested Hen.

"They don't usually operate with more than four."

"That's pretty good odds." Hen was thinking of escape. "One of them may be Prof W."

"There's a proper boatman - the helmsman knows what he's doing," confirmed Tom. "And I saw Wood with the drugs. There's the van driver, too - if he came... And what about Padget, himself? If so, that's five."

"We need a plan," murmured Hen. "This is our chance - five versus five at the most."

Tom called attention to the size of the hold. There was only so long they could be kept down there - it was too stuffy. He doubted the intention was to go very far.

"You're right. The oxygen will only last so long," agreed Hen.

Alice stirred and Tom bent to reassure her. "Hi, Alice. It's OK."

"W... What? Where are we?" she stammered.

"On a fishing boat," explained Hen

"That will explain why the floor is moving up and down... Ugh, it stinks," she groaned.

Tom passed her the piece of shell. "Scallops,"

"What are *they*?" asked Alice, still half-awake. "What's a

scallop?"

"The French call them *Noix de Saint Jacques*," answered Tom. "Very nice - pricey. You might recognise the whole shell." He splayed his fingers out to indicate it's size and shape. "It was used as a sign for pilgrimages."

"Oh, I know the one you mean," said Alice, coming to properly. "Like a fan. I've seen them on the walls in France to indicate the way to Santiago in Spain."

"You've got it. *Sant Iago* - *Saint Jacques* - Saint James," said Tom, glad to contribute some of his French knowledge. On a boat, he was feeling more at home, more himself. Alice took note and liked it. She smiled and their eyes met, momentarily. It made up for the discomfort of the heaving floor.

7

Nadia was next to stir. "Yuk!" Nadia was giving her first impressions of their latest prison. "Stinks, don't it?"

Alice explained. "Fish. You OK?" Just as Roxanne came to and groaned.

"I ain't," she grunted. "I feel sick. Where can I puke? Ugh... Gotta get out of here!"

"You are correct," said Hen. "We have to get out of here. But try and keep still. Now we are all awake we can make a plan."

"Better work better than the last one," muttered Nadia.

"Never any guarantees... And this time, if there is any explaining to do, leave it to me," said Hen.

Nadia was indignant."Are you saying it was my fault that we got caught again?"

"No. Not exactly..."

"What then?" Nadia became aggressive. Her head was clearing and she was both uncomfortable and scared.

Alice intervened. "Nadia. *All for one*... Let's look on the bright side; this time it *will* work. You have a plan, Hen?"

"No, not really. Tom, do you reckon we could overpower four men?"

"It'll be a problem. We can only get out of here one by one."

"A straight answer... and a logical one," sighed Hen, acknowledging the difficulties.

Tom went on; this was his environment. "We could dispose of one, maybe two if we surprise them, but they'll be bigger than us. And they'll probably be armed. But I only said they *usually* have a crew of no more than four. There could be more."

"More... or fewer," muttered Hen, thoughtfully.

"OK," said Roxanne, "so we've gotta be cunning. Why don't you tell them you'll change sides if they let you out. Tell them you have suddenly begun to see the world from their point of view. After all, that woman back there thought you had the breeding - whatever that means."

"Yeah," agreed Nadia, "They want *my* brain, not yours, don't they? Tell them you'll help them get it but they have to let me out to keep me healthy."

"Nadia that's ... that's brilliant," smiled Tom.

"I'm not all looks, mate. It's what Hen did at the Winterford, innit? He acted up to Prof W - they already think he's a spy."

"Yeah. That's right," agreed Alice, again. "That could just

work."

"Then," continued Nadia, "you jump out and tell them they have to leave the hatch open - to keep us healthy, like. Then you push one of them overboard, like, accidentally, and that'll make one less and we could all get out and tackle the rest."

"*Fewer*," corrected Hen. Nadia glared at him, wondering what he was on about. "One fewer..."

"Whatever!" retorted Nadia.

Alice stood up, looked Hen in the eye and extended a hand in Nadia's direction. She couldn't stand a fall-out - she knew it was the drugs and the stuffiness. "Please don't argue," she begged.

Hen apologised immediately. "Sorry, Nadia. That was rude of me. Lack of oxygen... Sorry... Your plan is a good one. I mean it." Nadia backed off.

"It might work but what if he drowned?" ventured Alice.

"Shucks to that!" spat Nadia, getting cross again. "They're set on killing us, ain't they? It's either them or us."

Tom was uneasy. "Still too slow, though. Especially if they've got that shotgun."

"Nadia's got the right idea, though" put in Roxanne. "If you made it look like an accident, they'll stop to pick him up and, while they're concentrating on doing that, we can all sneak out and rush the others. Don't worry, Alice, once we have control of the boat we can throw him a lifebuoy."

Hen was doubtful. "Still risky."

"Can you think of a better plan?" asked Roxanne.

"No. And the time is running short. We don't know where they're taking us and we could arrive before we act. And, in any case, we're getting far too short of air... OK. Say your prayers Rox... and you Nadia. You're good at them."

Nadia laughed, "It's OK, Hen. I ain't falling out with you... honest. God, make Hen a good actor, cheat, liar and despicable traitor. Amen... Oh and God," she added, "make him brave. Amen."

Hen had sinned but was now forgiven. "Thanks, Nadia."

"You're welcome."

Hen put his foot on the base of the short ladder. "Right. All lie down and look sick."

"No problem," grunted Roxanne.

Hen rapped on the underside of the hatch and shouted, "Hey, it's stuffy in here."

After a minute of shouting, a gruff voice replied - Wood's? "Shut up and keep quiet."

"Look, you don't understand," yelled Hen. "I'm on your side. Get the professor, he'll tell you."

He heard the man's footsteps along the deck. So the prof

was on board. Prof W approached and spoke through the hatch.

"What's all this, Christopher? What's this about being on my side?"

"Look, you know I always have been. I didn't understand until today and heard what that woman at the castle had to say. I share your politics. If we can use the fifth dimension to overcome the lack of discipline in the world... Get rid of all the weak stuff and divert our resources away from fluffy caring for the imperfect and subnormal people, we can begin to make real progress. Science and order, that's what we need... But right now, I have to get out of here because the air is getting foul. And we also need to preserve the health of the others or your experiments will be compromised. I am worried. They should have recovered from the drugs like me, but they are still too groggy. Nadia's pulse is erratic."

"Can I trust you, Christopher?"

"You have to if you want the plan to work."

That's neat, thought Alice, *The plan - I get it. Clever. Our Hen would really make a good spy. Or,* she thought, *write a book called, "How to lie without actually lying".*

Prof W gave an order and the hatch was opened. Hen felt the blast of fresh salty air and it was great. He climbed two rungs and put his head through the opening, turned and checked the deck. There was Wood and Prof W and just one more in the wheelhouse. Three. They were in luck. With his hand down by his side, he extended three fingers for the others to see and then gave them the thumbs up. The plan might just work.

Hen climbed the last few rungs, watching the sea. He hesitated, making out he was unsteady. After all, he was supposed to be recovering from the drugs and being cooped up below, wasn't he? And the boat was pitching. Wood stood to leeward. He was big and tall and his centre of gravity was well above the gunwale on the starboard side. Hen waited until he saw a wave that would tip the boat to his left. With a lunge, he pushed himself off the final rung and sideways into Wood who was caught unawares and stepped backwards, struck the gunwale with his calf and toppled overboard with a scream.

"Oh, crikey!" yelled Hen, "Sorry... Can we pick him up?"

The man in the wheelhouse had already slowed the engines and was spinning the wheel. The boat shuddered as it came side on to a wave and the next thing Prof W knew was that he, too, was in the water. Realising what was afoot, the captain left the cockpit and headed aft.

Nadia emerged from the hold and immediately spotted where he was going. The shotgun. She charged across the deck. The startled man reached for the gun just as Nadia grabbed at him. He didn't stand a chance as Nadia pulled him back and Roxanne was up next; she took the weapon in both hands and threw it into the sea.

"Great stuff, Rox," cried Alice, who had just got her head out of the hatch. "That's where we should chuck all the weapons in the world." She joined Nadia and Roxanne as the man scrambled off the washboard and stood with his hands in the air. He was hopelessly outnumbered; and this wasn't his fight. His immediate thought must have been for his boat which was still out of control in a not so calm ocean. But he needn't have worried. Tom had instinctively headed for the wheelhouse and was already taking control. He gently pulled the boat around into the swell.

Hen spotted Prof W coming up for the third time and threw him a lifebelt. The sea wasn't so cold that he would not survive for a few hours. Then Tom saw Wood swimming for an island but it would have been touch and go whether or not he made it – they didn't know the tides in this area. Tom pursued him and threw him a raft.

Hen consulted Tom about radioing a message. But the radio appeared to be out – it seemed the captain hadn't wanted anyone to know about this trip.

Hen joined the girls. They were making sure the captain

remained seated on the deck with his back to a coaming. Alice noticed his gaze. He was looking seawards in the direction of a large white yacht a couple of kilometres off.

"We could head towards that ship," shouted Tom. "That land there could be an island and I can't see a harbour."

"I don't like the look of that boat, Tom," returned Alice. "I reckon that's where we were headed in the first place. Am I right, captain?"

The man's look betrayed it all.

It was then that they saw a small craft coming towards them from the ship.

"Run, Tom," ordered Hen. "They've spotted our takeover."

"Right." shouted Tom. "Here we go." He turned the boat and fled towards the island at full-speed.

Alice found a length of rope. "Better tie you up, captain. Sorry," she said. "Hen, give us a hand." But the man proffered his wrists. There was no way he wanted to be thrown overboard too, and he knew that the five of them could do that easily. They tied his wrists and his ankles.

"You really know how to handle this thing," grinned Nadia, impressed with the way Tom managed the waves at speed.

"It's not a bad boat, but it isn't fast. And this sea isn't that calm," he answered, frustrated with his progress.

They were running against the current and after ten minutes they could see that the boat following them was an inflatable dingy that was much lighter in the water. There were at least five, possibly six men on board it.

At the police station in London, the Met were following up a lead. Sifting through the data history on the professor's computer, they noticed that a name came up fairly frequently – an American called Donald Padget.

8

Tom shouted from the wheelhouse. "I'm going to head around the point of the island. See if I can find a harbour. We'll never outrun them to the mainland. Not a chance."

"You know what they want to do to us?" began Nadia, looking daggers at the trussed up captain. "They—"

"Let Hen explain," broke in Alice.

Nadia looked up and was about to protest, but Hen began to do his best to put the situation to the captain less bluntly than Nadia would have.

"The thing is, we five have a rare condition – a kind of unusual ability – that might be useful to people set on destroying our free society. The professor, one of those in the water, has found himself in thrall to an extreme right-wing terrorist organisation in their quest to dominate the world. It is an organisation that has no sympathy with the needs of any individual. I would love to rescue him but we can't afford to be taken to the white boat. They are using far more sophisticated methods than merely mindless acts of terrorism and, therefore, ultimately, pose a far greater threat. We believe that the people on that big expensive yacht out there form part of the network. What they want with us is to examine us first alive and then dead."

"Especially dead!" a frustrated Nadia burst in. "They want to chop our heads off and slice up our brains – especially mine for some reason."

"My friend puts it rather crudely," smiled Hen, "but that's exactly what they want. So you can see why we need to avoid capture again."

The captain nodded. Whether it was Hen's reasoned style, Nadia's bluntness, the gentle manner in which Alice had gone about about tying him up, the impressive way Tom was handling his boat, or simply because he liked these young people, whatever the reason he agreed to be on their side. He hadn't liked the way that they had been treated from the start.

"Go passed this point," he called. "There's a shoal 200 yards from those rocks so don't take it too tightly, and then around the far headland. There's no proper beach on this side at all; the island's been uninhabited since the 1930s, but you can try and hide among the trees and stuff... if you let me have my boat after you're on the island, I'll carry on going – cause a diversion."

"Thanks. But they'll catch you," shrugged Alice.

"Yes and I'll tell them I'm going back to look for the men in the sea. You made me take you to the island – that'll be no lie... There's water on the island - a stream in the gully. No food mind. By the time they find you, I'll be home and I promise I'll raise the alarm."

"Tell the police?" Alice asked.

"The coastguard."

"Perfect," said Hen. "That's exactly what we want you to do. I think we can untie the gentleman, Alice."

They found the beach and the captain let Tom take them in. They hadn't seen the dinghy since they'd rounded the first headland but it couldn't be far away. Hen checked through some binoculars he had found on board.

"Can I keep these?" Hen asked, holding them up. "I promise I'll get them back to you when this is over."

"Fine. Take them," answered the fisherman, although he very much doubted whether he would see the young people again. However he was going to talk his way out of the disaster the trip had turned out to be he had no idea. He took over from Tom and drew as near to the breaking waves as he could.

"Not up the beach!" yelled Hen as the youngsters leapt over the side into the surf. "We mustn't leave footprints in the sand. Let's head along to those rocks, keeping in the water."

As they waded towards the rocky headland, they heard the captain put his boat into reverse and head out to sea. They had only just scrambled up onto a pile of rocks on the side of the headland when they registered the sound of an outboard motor. Instinctively they ducked down among the rock pools – not even Nadia was curious enough to peak over her rock to see what was happening. From where they were hiding they heard the inflatable's buzz ricocheting off the cliffs - amplified by the entrance to a vast cavern behind them. The craft passed and the sounds diminished. Tom looked up carefully.

"They're chasing the boat; he's heading round the next point where they'll be out of sight."

Alice watched between the rocks as the fast inflatable pursued the captain. She sighed. "He's a good man. He wants to give us a chance... I hope nothing awful happens to him."

"It's the first time anyone's believed us," said Nadia, as they quickly made their way along a line of stones to a stand of trees behind the beach. "I ain't saying that I couldn't have convinced him by myself but I have to admit you did a good job, Hen." She looked at him with a reluctant smile.

"Thanks," he said, genuinely moved. Somehow a compliment from Nadia, even a grudging one, really meant something. He couldn't remember getting one from her before – not so directly given, anyway. "I appreciate that... Teamwork."

From that moment onwards, he and Nadia connected in a

way that was not so much on a words level - his vocabulary was twice hers - but based on some deeper mutual respect. Nadia found herself trusting him - really trusting him. Like she trusted Alice for not running away and Rox for befriending her.

9

The five friends made their way through the trees which stretched up from the beach, and climbed a gully lined with ferns and mosses. A tinkling sound indicated a hidden trickle of water. The sun was warm. They sat on a rock to rest and dry their legs.

"This is like an adventure of *The Famous Five*," suggested Alice.

"Who are they?" asked Nadia.

"It's a series of stories by Enid Blyton," explained Alice.

Nadia smirked. "Noddy?"

"Same author, but Noddy doesn't come into it."

Hen suggested another story. "Defoe – *Robinson Crusoe*. That book might prove useful here."

Alice puckered up her nose. "Nah. It's too long... and boring." But then something occurred to her. "Just a minute, Hen. Is that where you got the no-footprints-in-the-sand idea from? They knew Friday was there from his footprint."

"Maybe. I wasn't thinking about it."

Roxanne was lost. "What on earth are you lot talking

about? I don't know nothing about books," she said. "What I'm reminded of is *Castaway* – the film... WILSON!!" she bellowed, at the top of her lungs. It was an excellent imitation of Tom Hanks.

They all laughed – it felt good. It was possible to feel safe and free in the shelter of the trees. Alice sensed a flip coming on but she was determined to resist it. She looked down the gully to check if anyone was around to have heard them, and just the slightest thought that they might have, resulted in sufficient anxiety to stop it. She grabbed hold of Tom next to her who was also about to go and said firmly.

"No, Tom, better not." Alice caught Hen's gaze and he, too, gained control. Roxanne, alone, was unmoved. It would take more than the delight of freedom in a wooded grove to send her flipping.

Between them, they took hold of Nadia who was on the point of slumping forward. She wasn't gone long. Alone in the fifth, she had pushed herself to re-enter the vortex as soon as it appeared.

When they had recovered, Alice described how she had avoided going. It was her genuine concern about being discovered by Padget that she had tapped into. That would not always apply, but it was a start. For Hen, control was key.

Climbing further up, they came to the end of the trees. Alice took the binoculars and scrambled a little higher until she had a view out to sea. She could see both sides of their island and the white yacht some distance away. She spotted the two craft – the fishing boat and the dinghy – bobbing together on the waves. A puff of exhaust appeared from the fishing boat as its engines started. It turned back towards the mainland, away from the big white yacht – if the dinghy crew had let the captain go, it would only be a matter of time before someone knew where they were. Alice climbed back down to the others and described what she had seen.

Nadia cheered. "So the coastguard'll come and rescue us."

Hen was more cautious. "Maybe. We don't know who's in the boat, though."

"What about the prof?" asked Alice. "Will they rescue him?"

"And Wood," murmured Hen. "I hope so." It had been he who had shouldered them over the rail.

Tom was sure they would be all right. "This island is the shape of a diamond. It was when we had the island to starboard that we ditched them. If they make it ashore, they'll be down there on the other side from where we landed. If they're still in the water... I'm sure the captain'll look for them...

Pity the radio was disabled."

"Won't he know how to turn it on?" wondered Alice.

Tom shrugged. "Seemed dead to me. No power at all. But they had a lifebelt and a raft. He'll find them."

"Maybe," said Hen, half to himself, "or maybe not. The boat is not forced to be piloted by the captain; we haven't seen the full encounter. And rescuing people demands compassion - something the fascist hard-line philosophy excludes."

Hen assumed the lead. Back in this world, Rox was not saying much at all. "OK. So we have to assume we will be here for a few hours at least. We need to find water before it gets dark."

"And something to eat," added Nadia. "If possible...?"

Hen sprang up. "There may be something, but I don't think we're going to get a feast. It's about keeping alive, not satisfying our hunger."

"But in that cave we saw," joked Alice, "there could be heaps of tins left over from the second world war..."

Hen applauded her positive attitude and replied playfully. "Alice, this *isn't* the *Famous Five*! It only works like that in children's stories."

"And this in't a children's story," grumbled Nadia.

"But it's a much nicer story than it was a couple of hours

ago," Roxanne reassured her. "I can live without food for a bit if I am free."

"And that's the plan," affirmed Hen. "We are and with a bit of luck we'll remain so. It's just a matter of time before someone comes looking for us."

Alice was determined to look on the bright side. "And they'll already be asking questions in London."

Hen agreed and reminded them of their ally in New York. "And I am sure Bishop Rowena will act on our may-day."

But Nadia was determined to be realistic. She was tired, too. "From New York! She hardly knows us!"

Hen was forced to agree. Bishop Rowena was a long shot.

"The people in the inflatable must know we're here on this island," Tom reminded them. "Where else could we have gone to? They'll come looking for us. It's a question of when and if we can hold out until help arrives."

Almost at the same moment, they heard the sound of an outboard motor. Alice's heart plummeted. Tom's face fell. "It seems they're already circling the island looking for us."

Hen clung onto hope. "But it's not that small and it'll soon be dark. If we can hold out until then, we have a chance."

Eventually, as the sun sank lower in the sky, they heard the sound of the outboard motor recede and fade out of earshot.

Unbeknown to the young people, the fishing vessel was not being returned to the mainland by its captain – he was deemed to know too much. It was being taken to the open sea many miles to the south where it was to be abandoned – the captain having been transferred into the inflatable.

Sadly, as Hen had predicted, the people from the white yacht had no intention of wasting time and effort looking for Prof W and Wood.

10

Having drunk from a little spring at the top of the gully, the five decided they would explore the island for food. The island was indeed diamond-shaped – probably no more than a mile long at its longest point – but it was big enough to give them a chance to hide from a search party. And the fact that it was tree-covered in parts, with broken and rocky ground elsewhere, would also help. On the far side, the young people spotted what looked like a dry stone wall and they decided to check it out. It was broken but they could clearly see that it had once enclosed a piece of flat ground.

"This could have been built to keep animals in," speculated Tom.

"Or out; there may have been a garden here," suggested Roxanne.

She was right. Tom recognised potato plants and parsnips among the grass, together with some stunted fruit trees. Roxanne found a stick and grubbed around the base of one of the plants revealing beautiful cream-coloured potatoes. Soon, they had a decent pile as well as parsnips and some huge scabby looking carrots. Then Nadia turned around with a red-stained smile. She had found what she proclaimed were raspberries.

"That was daring of you," observed Alice. "They could have been poisonous."

"They didn't look poisonous. And they ain't. Try one."

"A loganberry," pronounced Tom. "A cross between a raspberry and a blackberry. They're delicious. Our problem with the potatoes is that they need cooking, and cooking needs a fire, and fire means smoke. We'll have to wait until it's dark or be sure the white yacht has gone before we light one."

"We could use smoke to signal for help," suggested Alice.

Hen disagreed. "The white yacht people will be here much sooner than anyone from the mainland. They know we're on the island and they might be content to wait until tomorrow to come looking for us. If we draw attention to ourselves we might spook them into action. For now, we can eat carrot; it might not be very tender but you can eat it raw."

They took their haul back to the spring and washed the vegetables. Hen tried taking a bite of a carrot. It was hard, woody and not very sweet, but it was more than edible. He passed it to Alice who took a bite, too. "Hardly cordon bleu, she pronounced. "But when you're hungry..." They devoured the root between them. Great. Loganberries and carrot! With food inside them, their spirits lifted.

"If we feel short of protein," pronounced Hen, "we could eat worms."

"Yuk!" scowled Roxanne. "I'm not *that* hungry!"

"Or we could catch fish," suggested Tom. "If they leave us here, with this water and this stuff we could stay healthy for quite a while."

"Hanks was on his island for four years," muttered Nadia.

"Yes. But that was in the tropics where there was no autumn or winter," responded Alice. "And I sincerely hope we won't have to last out that long."

"If the yacht clears off we can light a huge fire with lots of smoke which will easily be seen across the straight," put in Roxanne. "Tom Hank's island was in the middle of the Pacific miles from anywhere but we won't need four days, let alone four years."

"The only problem is the baddies," sighed Nadia. "Tom Hanks didn't have any of them to contend with... I wish they would just go away."

Roxanne, tried to look on the bright side. "Let's hope they do. They might decide we're not worth all the effort – or they could be scared of being caught if they hang around."

Hen was doubtful. "Maybe."

Alice wanted to be realistic. All this stuff about books and films was getting to her. These people were dangerous. "But let's be honest, guys; they won't, will they?" All of a sudden she felt tired as the enormous truth hit her. "The trouble is we know too much. Padget, Inverlochie - we can dob them all in, and they know it. They can't afford to give up on us."

11

The sun sank below the horizon as the five sat together on the summit of their island nibbling carrots. Alice began thinking of the way they had dumped Wood and the professor overboard. They hadn't had much choice – if they hadn't escaped, they would be on their way to the prof's scientific facilities. He might even have what he needed to begin his experiments on board that luxury yacht. All the same, the thought that two people might have drowned was not a pleasant one.

About an hour later, however, they heard a distinct moan from the rocks below them.

"Weird sound," whispered Nadia, "is that a seal or something?"

"No," supplied Tom. "Or at least not a variety that I recognise."

They heard it again.

Roxanne sat up. "That's no animal; it's human." Alice shivered.

"Could be Prof W," suggested Hen, "or Wood. He was

swimming this way. If they weren't picked up, they could have made the rocks down there."

They heard the groan again – distinctly weaker this time. A bright moon lit their way as they climbed down to where the sound appeared to be coming from.

Eventually, they found its origin; it was indeed their professor. He was in a really bad way. Barely conscious, he raised his right arm and then let it fall.

The young people stood and stared. "What are we going to do?" murmured Alice; she was confused and felt helpless.

"He'll need water," said Roxanne, instinctivley taking the lead in mdical matters and stepping forward to examine him. "I doubt he's had anything to drink since he left the boat."

"We'll probably kill him trying to take him to the spring," despaired Alice but Hen began scouring the tide line among the driftwood and flotsam left by the tide. At last, he found what he was looking for – a plastic bottle. For once, the plastic-polluted seas had come in handy. Nadia grabbed it from him. "I'll get some water from the spring."

"You know the way, Nadia?" asked Hen.

"Course. Me, I never get lost."

The professor fell into total unconsciousness as the remaining four lifted him off the rocks and onto a flat piece of rough grass studded with daisies and other sweet-smelling flowers. Alice noticed the daisies and it got her thinking. "You know, if he were truly one of them he would have a daisy somewhere, wouldn't he?"

"Yeah," said Tom. "But I've never seen one on him anywhere."

Hen reckoned that their professor had got caught up in this because the daisy group had taken advantage of his financial fragility. "And now they're threatening him with his life, too. And, I guess, once they've got what they want they'll get rid of him."

"Kill him?!" exclaimed Alice.

"They're not going to let him free to split on them any more than they would us," sighed Roxanne. "Like us, Alice, he knows too much. Left to himself, I doubt he would ever kill anyone to experiment on. Would you, professor?"

But the professor was not with it. Tom gathered a bunch of beech leaves and wiped the man's face. His clothes were sodden and heavy with salt water.

"Should we take his wet things off?" asked Alice.

"No," said Roxanne, "we shouldn't remove his clothes unless we have something warm and dry to cover him with. Better leave them on." She checked Prof W's limbs one at a time. "Nothing broken. He's a bit scraped in places, but the cuts aren't deep."

Nadia returned with the water at double quick time. She might not have outrun Alice on the track, but she was pretty sure-footed over stones and through brambles by moonlight.

"Brilliant," congratulated Hen, "You were quick."

Nadia smiled."Course. I found a stream closer than the spring."

They wet the professor's lips and washed his face, which was pretty badly sunburned. Roxanne felt his pulse; it was reasonably strong.

The professor now gained some sort of consciousness and he managed a few sips of the water. Then he went to sleep. This time it seemed like true sleep, not unconsciousness.

Alice decided to rummage among the flotsam further along the beach in search of more intact bottles. She was amazed at all the plastic – they weren't joking when they said about there being as much plastic in the ocean as fish. But unbroken bottles were an asset at that moment. She judged that they would have to stay with Prof W – they couldn't go back to the gully to spend the night and leave him and they would all need water. She had just found a second bottle – a nice large one – when she spotted a heap of something among the seaweed. It was only a dark shape on the shingle amongst the seaweed but there was no mistaking it. It was a body. Wood?

"Hey, guys," she called. "Over here."

Hen was the first to join her. She indicated the body.
"Dead? Is he dead?"

12

Hen took a couple of paces towards the body and softly ordered, "Get Rox." Alice went back to where Tom and Roxanne were still bending over their professor.

"Another... body," she indicated. "Hen wants your opinion, Dr Tom."

Tom stood up, "Wood?"

"Don't know for sure. Probably. Big man."

It was Wood. Hen was looking for a pulse in a wrist swathed in seaweed. Roxanne arrived and found the left carotid artery with two fingers.

"He's alive. But only just."

Wow! Hen felt so much relief he was on the point of flipping. "O...? Only just?" he stammered. Wood had been mean and uncaring. He knew exactly what the brain plan was and he had seemed to enjoy himself throwing his weight around. The only bit he didn't enjoy was being bested in a fight. To say he was an unsavoury character was an understatement. But despite all this Hen was truly relieved – he had not killed him ... well, the man hadn't died yet.

"He's pretty sick," pronounced Roxanne. "He's barely breathing. I think he's got water in his lungs. We need to get him on his front, head down the slope."

"It'll need all of us to lift him. Where shall we put him?"

They examined a few sites and found a place which Roxanne declared was flat enough. "If we can get him up here."

"Where there's a will, there's way," affirmed Hen.

They were silent before Nadia asked, "Is he going to die?"

"Not if we can help it," stated Tom. "Give us a hand will you?"

"Like, without killing him in the process," sneered Nadia. "He's dangerous, this one."

"Let's carry him feet-first so his head is downhill," suggested Tom.

Tom took the head and shoulders and asked Hen to take the man's bottom. "We don't want to tip the water back into his lungs. Nadia, Rox can you help with the legs? Yes. Alice, help Hen in the middle. That's it. On the count of three. One, two, three, lift."

They manhandled the dead weight over the lip of the grassy sward and lowered him gently onto the turf. Tom wanted them to turn him over.

"Get his right leg over the top of his left... Great. Now roll."

Following Roxanne's directing, they rolled over the heavy man more easily than they thought they would and a gush of sea-water came out of the his mouth.

"Great," said Tom. "We might just have done the trick." They laid him in a prone position with his head slightly downhill. Already his breathing seemed better. Roxanne felt his pulse again. It was much stronger. "I reckon the ox is going to live," she smiled.

"What happens when he wakes up?" wondered Nadia.

"We'll tell him we saved his life," said Hen, calmly. "At least Rox has. I shoved him in; Rox saved him. He's a lucky man."

Roxanne dismissed the compliment. "Joint effort."

13

After a quarter of an hour, Wood was regaining some sort of consciousness. Nadia grew anxious; the beast was stirring. But he did not wake up. Other than a few noises that indicated that he was not going to die – at least not immediately – Wood lay still, exactly where the five had placed him.

"I'm pooped," said Nadia. "If you lot don't mind I'm going over there by that tree and I am going to the land of Nod... Here, I found another bottle."

"That's fantastic," said Hen. "You go and sleep. We'll have to take turns with watching over our patients. I'll go and wash and fill this bottle and put it by your side."

"There's a gully on this side of the island," said Nadia, "just beyond the wall. You don't have to go all the way back to the first one. Look, you won't find it in the dark. Let me go. I'll wash there and then come back. Then I'm going to bed down here," she was making quite a nice bed of sweet-smelling beech leaves to lie on.

"You can eat them," explained Tom. "They're beech."

"Great. So if I get peckish, I'll have a nibble of my bed,"

she laughed. Then she was gone, picking her way through the stones in the starlight. Alice and Roxanne called after her and caught her up.

"Show us where. I could do with washing, too. I can feel the salt on my skin and it's beginning to hurt," complained Alice.

"My hair's worse," grumbled Roxanne. "Haven't washed it for ages... Reckon the boys will think I'm gross."

"Doubt it. We're all the same. Besides, if we're gross what about them?" laughed Alice.

Back with the beech leaves, Hen asked Tom, "You want to wash when the girls get back?"

"I suppose. Can't rightly say I'd thought about it. Too busy."

"I'm going to leave it until morning," sighed Hen. "Nadia won't want to make another trip in the dark to show us where."

"Good idea. Let me take the first watch," offered Tom. "I'll wake you when the moon is up."

"Rox, you saved Wood's life. He was dying."

"Yup. I thought he was a goner, too. We were lucky with the water coming out like that."

"It wasn't all luck, Tom. You worked with gravity. I wouldn't have thought of the feet up bit."

"It was... well, it just seemed like common sense. I wasn't expecting anything other than not making it worse."

"Well, whatever. You saved him... Thanks." Hen spoke with earnest.

"Why so pleased? He's a monster."

"I know. But I was the one who pushed him over the side of the boat. If he dies, it will always be on my conscience."

"It was us or them... and we all agreed to the plan," stated Tom, emphatically.

"I know. But I still have a heart. I guess it wouldn't quite be guilt – but not far off it."

"You mean, Hen, you knew what you did was justified, so you know in your *head* that you aren't guilty but in your *heart*..."

"In my heart, I would know that I had killed a man."

"Don't go into the army, Hen."

"You're right... You know, before this happened, that was one of the options open to me. Clearly, it would have been a mistake. But the armed forces are out now anyway. What, with 5D and all."

Tom looked up at the stars. He was thinking of his own future, too. "I guess so. What about being a politician?"

"No. You have to belong to a political party. I couldn't belong to any of them."

"Bishop, then? Like Bishop Rowena? You'd make a good bishop."

The girls returned refreshed and Hen excused himself. Explaining that Tom was taking the first watch, he would go and "water a patch of grass" and make a bed on the other side of the tree.

It wasn't long before all four were asleep.

An hour later, Wood stirred and semi-consciously pulled himself round so that he was head up the slope. Tom watched him fall back again, then approached him. "Water?" he asked. Wood grunted, opened his mouth and drank; then subsided again. *By morning you might become a handful,* Tom thought. *But we'll be ready for you.*

14

A hazy sun appeared above a distant range of mountains on the mainland. Alice pulled herself up from her bed of leaves and ferns and examined the scene around her. She was damp with dew. How had she slept so soundly and for so long? She staggered over to where Hen sat propped against a rock. He was asleep but woke with a start as Alice approached.

"Must have dozed off," he apologised. Wood and Prof W were still prone.

"They alive?"

"Were when I last looked."

Alice went over to the professor. He opened his eyes.

"You OK?"

"S... sorry," he stammered. He tried to sit and fell back.

"Better get you under that tree. The sun will soon be on this place. You had too much of it yesterday."

Nadia had awoken too and was eating beech leaves. They were stringy at that time of year but tasted OK. She became aware of Roxanne who seemed to be sobbing quietly.

"You OK, Rox?"

"Yeah." She sat up and blew her nose on a soggy handkerchief.

"Look, Rox. We ain't going to be sleeping outside for the rest of our lives."

"No. It ain't that."

"What then?"

"Nothing."

"You miss him, don't you?"

"Miss who?"

"I ain't daft, Rox. That lad in the resistance."

"Yeah. I miss him. I miss them all. They were a kind of family."

"You never had a proper family on this side, did you? You're like me, only worse. My old man might be a pain, but he doesn't abuse me."

"I ain't never going back to where I came from in this world, Nadia."

"I don't blame you, and you don't have to. You can come and live with me – forever. I would like that. And you belong to the 5D family now. I mean the others might be a bit clever and posh but they're real and would protect you with their lives. 'One for all and all for one' ain't no joke. They could all have run off when I got grabbed at the bottom of that mountain, but they didn't. And they'd do the same for you. We all would."

Roxanne crawled over to Nadia and gave her a hug.

"Give over the emotional, will ya," whispered Nadia into Roxanne's ear. "Look you belong, OK. I mean it. When we get back to normal you can come and live with me."

"Thanks, Nadia. But when this is all over I'm going back - to the flipside."

"Well, there's one thing I can say for you, Roxanne, you're brave - a lot braver than me."

Hen called a powwow under a tree out of earshot of the two prone men.

"You can bring your breakfast with you, Nadia."

"You want some, Hen?"

"Not after you've been sleeping on it!" he retorted, playfully.

"It's a lot cleaner than what your stuff is. At least, I had a proper wash last night!" Nadia teased in return.

Under a tree, where the "enemy" as they called them couldn't overhear, they thought about the day. Wood was not going to be a problem, Hen reckoned; even if he felt more like it, he would lack the inclination to do anything but lay around. They decided that Hen and Nadia should go to the top of the island and check if the big white yacht had moved on. If it had, they would light a signal fire and cook potatoes at the same time. The others were to get Wood and the professor properly under the cover of the trees out of the sun, which was already becoming quite strong; it was going to be a hot day.

Fifteen minutes later, Hen and Nadia came bounding back down the hill. The white yacht was still holding its station and the inflatable with at least four men aboard was headed towards the island. There was no way they could draw attention to themselves – so no fires. They would have to make do with leaves and berries again.

"Cave dwellers food again," mumbled Alice. "Where are we going to hide?"

"Among the trees," directed Hen. "We'll be able to see them, but they won't see us. We'll just have to keep moving. We have the advantage if we're clever. The longer it takes them to catch us, the more chance of someone coming and finding us first."

Alice didn't share his optimism but decided not to say anything.

Hen's statement about having the advantage was quickly contradicted. As soon as the men got off the boat, they launched a drone.

"Should have guessed," groaned Hen, as they heard the

thing top the hill above them. It sounded like a swarm of angry bees.

The five kept low beneath the trees but it was onto them within minutes.

"Infrared?" suggested Tom.

"Maybe," shrugged Hen. "Whatever its eyes, it can definitely see us."

It hovered above them like a giant bird of prey. Angry, Roxanne picked up a stone and threw it in its direction. "Brilliant idea!" said Nadia. "All we need is a catapult."

"Why? Can you use one?" asked Tom.

"Course."

Tom took off his belt. "This do?"

"Hey. Yeah!" said Nadia. It was just the thing.

Nadia found a stone a couple of centimetres in diameter and put it in a loop of Tom's belt. It only missed by a couple of metres. She barely had time to regain her balance before Tom thrust another stone into her hand. They kept her plied with ammunition and on the eighth or ninth attempt she hit it. It swerved and then swooped and fell. They ran to where it lay and Tom heaved as big a rock as he could find and smashed it. After it was clearly not going anywhere or seeing anything, Hen called on them all to run. They needed to get as far as they could from the site of the crash. Now the advantage was theirs again.

"Nadia, you're a star!" declared Hen.

"I know," crowed Nadia.

"Cave dwellers one, state-of-the-art tech, nil," laughed Tom.

"What if we flipped into the flipside?" suggested Roxanne. "I mean we would be safe there. We could wait on this island for a day or two – it's bound to be the same as here. Then we could come back and signal after the yacht has gone."

"That might work," said Tom.

Hen became the thoughtful realist. "I'm not sure. First, we do not *know* the island would be the same. People clearly lived here in the past. On the flipside they might still be around and the last thing we want is to be caught by the Nazis. Here, we only have a few men in a white yacht to avoid."

Alice didn't want to get trapped somewhere where she was never going to be able to get home. "And, who knows," she said, "it could be crawling with soldiers – a base or something – and then we would be really stuffed. We flipped back and landed in a den of vipers last time. It could happen again."

"I think flipping's worth the risk," said Tom. "Alice, it would only be for two days."

"Well, OK," agreed Alice, reluctantly.

But Nadia was troubled. "What about Wood and the

professor. Will our hunters look after them if we leave?"

"Doubt it," said Roxanne. "Not if they're like the fascists I've met."

"If we escape, they won't have any use for Prof W," murmured Hen. "And Wood will have failed. So, to be honest, I wouldn't put their chances of survival very high. You've seen how ruthless these people can be."

Nadia was not willing to abandon two sick men – even if they had meant her harm. "We've saved them from dying – I reckon we have to see it through. But if the dudes in the dinghy turn out not to be mean and look after them, then I'm with Roxanne and will try and muster up a flip. But if they ignore them or worse, I can't see how we can leave them."

"Well argued," complimented Hen. "For now, we must wait and watch."

15

One of the detectives searching Prof W's filing cabinets in the Winterford office drew the attention of his colleagues to a financial statement he had discovered.

"Look at this. Our Mr Donald Padget virtually owns this place. That gentleman's put in nigh on two million pounds. The other income barely pays the electricity bill."

"Let's find out all we can about this Mr Padget," ordered the DI. "I have more than a hunch he's the one behind all this. Find him and we find the young people."

"And the professor?" asked the Detective Sergeant.

"And the professor, too," nodded his boss.

An unmarked police vehicle rolled up to Inverlochie Castle. The local detective inspector decided he must take this one himself. After all, Donald Padget was the laird – even if they didn't know much about him and he lived in America most of the time.

He was greeted by the friendly face of Audra McBlair. The detective introduced himself and she conducted him to her office. The laird was not in residence, she told him. Did he know he lived most of the time in America? The detective noticed that she didn't actually say where he was at that moment.

All through the interview, she put on an air of being as helpful as possible. Yes, as it happened, they had found some mentally disturbed teenagers - she didn't know their names. They must have run away from some institution and put themselves in considerable danger; they had been improperly dressed for the fells and were rather "wild". But they were nothing to do with the laird.

What had happened was that a tenant farmer had complained that five ill-disciplined teenagers whom he thought must have come from the castle - although they hadn't - had been damaging his pasture. They wanted to keep the farmer happy so they had gone out and collected them and brought them back to the castle where they had been given clean clothes.

Eventually, someone in a van had come looking for them and took them away - back to their institution, she supposed.

McBlair conducted the inspector to the bathrooms in which the young people had washed and changed but the rooms had been cleaned and the dirty clothes disposed of.

The inspector asked about the farmer who had found them and he left to interview him.

McBlair felt satisfied. She was sure the DI was treating the inquiry as routine. He had been polite to the point of being apologetic. She attempted to contact Padget, but the call wouldn't go through. She could only suppose that he was out of range - not unusual in the Highlands - or hadn't managed to replace his phone. She had put the shattered remains of the previous one in the bin - Nadia had done too good a job on it.

Comfortable that there had been nothing particularly unusual in five young people roaming the hills, the inspector followed McBlair's directions and drove up the valley.

"Aye," protested the farmer. "Traipsing all over the pasture they were as if it didn't matter. No country sense. Been out all night by the looks of it. Silly clothes for teenagers, too. They were the sort of things my parents might have worn when they were young in the 1950s - indoors. They didn't fit them either. They looked really odd."

The inspected was curious. "Do you know their names? I need to identify them. The Met in London are looking for some kids and thought they might have come up this way. I need to eliminate them from their inquiries."

"No. They didn't give their names. And I didn't ask. They been getting up to something? Mad bunch, them."

"I'm just trying to identify them," explained the DI.

"There were two lads and three girls – one of them was black... Yes. Oddly dressed for teenagers," continued the farmer.

The DI copied it all down in his notebook.

"And what is also odd is that they didn't try to put them in a car or a minibus but the back of a closed van. The kids refused the lift and walked away; they promised to keep to the road and they headed off down the lane. I thought that would be the end of it but when they got to the bend, the estate people caught up with them and tried to force them into the van. The kids put up a fight. The black one – she could swear like a trouper – kept yelling something about the prof not getting her brain. Really odd. Definitely mad... They got over the gate and charged across my grass again without a by-your-leave."

"Which way did they go?" asked the detective.

"They got to the wall over there and began to climb over but thought better of it when they saw Charlie."

The farmer did not make any mention of his shotgun.

"Charlie? Whose Charlie?"

"My bull."

"Ah! I see." The policeman was taking in the scene. "So what happened next?"

"They got 'em into the van and drove off."

"Can you describe this van?" asked the DI.

"Aye. It was a red Toyota. We don't get many like that around here. It belongs to the estate."

"Thank you," said the detective. "That's helpful."

As he got back into his car, the detective inspector phoned in to report that there had been five young people that had been disturbing the peace – three girls and two boys. One of the girls was black and had shouted a lot of obscenities and something about a professor not getting her brain. Other than that he had no names.

Ten minutes later the sergeant rang back. Apparently, the American laird also owned, in all but name, a clinic in London headed by a professor – a neuroscientist who, among other things, dissected brains. This professor had also disappeared.

"The Met suspects abduction," continued the sergeant. "They say the missing young people are almost certainly in real danger... If these are they, they'll be glad to hear they're still alive," he added.

The detective breathed deeply. He felt his body tighten.

"They were collected from the farm in a red Toyota van," he reported. "I saw no sign of the van at the castle. I want that van found. Join me with two uniformed constables at the castle. I don't have to emphasise that this has become serious." The DI had given his orders.

16

As the five friends circled the island keeping out of sight, they checked up on their professor and Wood as they passed. It looked as if the searchers had ignored them; they *must* have come across them. Hen said that he wasn't surprised. "You still want to hang around Nadia? It's you they have lined up for..." He didn't have to spell it out.

"Yeah. We have to stay - we can't leave them," affirmed Nadia. "It ain't right just leaving someone to die."

Hen was relieved. "Thanks."

Tom checked the area was safe and went across to the professor. "You being looked after?" he whispered.

Prof W shook his head.

Nadia gave him a handful of berries she had hoarded in a large leaf and swapped his empty bottle for hers. "Sorry," she said. "It's all we can do - no peace to fish or cook."

Prof W looked at her. The whites of his eyes were yellow. Alice didn't like the look of him. "You keeping me alive?" he asked Nadia.

"Course."

The professor's lips moved. "Love your enemies, do good to those who hate you," he murmured, almost inaudibly.

"You what?" said Nadia.

"N... Nothing... You go to church?" he whispered.

"Who me?" said Nadia, almost forgetting to keep her voice down. "Nah. Why? Oh, yeah... The youth club. That was Hen's idea. Anything to get an outing. Those guys were great, though. I would go back there to that club... Anyway, we can't hang around. Better eat and drink this. We'll be back. What about Wood?"

Alice and Tom had already moved on to him. He was in a bad way. They were trying to persuade him to drink. Roxanne came over. "He's dehydrated," she sighed. "He needs to be put on a drip."

"I wish these people would give up chasing us and begin looking after their own," sighed Alice. Hen and Nadia joined them.

"I couldn't agree more," said Hen. "I didn't intend to kill him."

"It ain't your fault," began Nadia, "It's just—"

She never finished her sentence. Looking up, they found themselves surrounded by four men in black, levelling rifles at them.

"Stand up!" barked one of them. They stood. "Your

adventures end here."

"Probably for the best," mumbled Hen. "Now perhaps you can give these people the care they need."

"Your own stupid social concern has caught you out. You might have got away if it weren't for your soft lovey-dovey hearts. Another hour and we would have given up."

"Would you have taken Prof W and Wood to safety?" asked Alice.

"Maybe."

"If you leave them here, they will die," declared Hen. "And then where will you be? After all, the professor here has all the knowledge. Worth keeping him alive, wouldn't you say?"

"Shut it! Enough talk. Get down to the boat!"

Hen went towards Wood. "Come on, Tom. I don't trust them not to leave their 'friends' to die... OK. Lower the gun," he said, looking the black-clad leader in the eye. "We're not going to take on the four of you armed as you are, are we? Someone'd be bound to get killed. But as I doubt you'll want to put your weapons aside to get your wounded to safety, you'd better let us do it."

Alice and Nadia held onto the professor's arms as they helped him struggle down to the rocks. Roxanne joined them as they took most of his weight and then lifted him into the inflatable.

"Sorry!" apologised Alice, and then added to the others, "Really needed a stretcher."

Ignoring the barked orders of the men in black, they returned to get Wood and all five heaved him down the beach. Seeing that they had little option, two of the men handed their guns to the others and helped to lift Wood carefully onto the bottom of the boat. They decided it was easier than dragging five reluctant teenagers whom they had orders to bring in unharmed.

When they were all crowded in the small craft, Nadia found herself jammed up against Wood's head. "Hope you're grateful," she mumbled. Wood was beyond making a reply; if he didn't receive care soon, it would be unlikely that he would say anything again.

Tom made sure he was next to Alice and put his arm around her. Her heart warmed. Whatever was going to happen to them, Alice knew he would stick by her.

17

The big white yacht was a floating mansion. She was more than thirty metres long and boasted the height of luxury. Wood and Prof W were hoisted aboard and taken off somewhere. Alice hoped it would be to be given the medical care which they so desperately needed.

The place destined to serve as a brig for all five young people was a small but comfortable inside cabin on a lower deck belonging to the ship's maintenance crew. The door was locked and a guard posted. As they heard an anchor stowed, the engines throb and the bows begin to slap against the waves, Nadia, Alice, Roxanne, Hen and Tom perched on bunks and wondered what they could possibly do to save themselves,

"We were stupid," bemoaned Alice. "They guessed we'd go back to see if Prof W and that oaf, Wood, were OK."

"Had no choice," shrugged Nadia. "Couldn't let them die, could we?"

Alice sighed. "Guess not. But Nadia, what's going to happen to us? I know I was reluctant, but if we'd done what Roxanne said and gone back to the flipside, we wouldn't have been caught."

"Look, I'd rather end up dead doing the right thing, than living doing the wrong thing," answered Nadia. "I couldn't have lived with that. And Hen would have died of guilt if Wood had snuffed it."

"It was *you* who wanted to save the prof—" began Hen, a little defensively.

"Look, you're both right and both brave," asserted Tom. "Doing the right thing isn't always safe."

That sparked Roxanne. "It's effing dangerous most of the time on the Nazi flipside. We may be in a fix here but that's just us. It's a darn sight nicer for most everybody else."

"If Padget gets his way, this side could become like that flipside," declared Alice. "If they get our brains and they use the knowledge they gain to overcome the world, then... well, we would have done more harm than good in getting caught."

"That isn't going to happen," put in Hen, confidently. "We all know that the professor's been barking up the wrong tree. Our brains are physiologically normal. He's put us through scan after scan and found nothing. However much research they do on us, it won't get them anywhere... And, besides, much cleverer or more powerful people in the past have tried to take over the world and they've all failed in the end. You only need to look at Genghis Khan, Bonaparte, and a plethora of other dictators. And we know that the flipside won't stay Nazi either – the people are against them. We witnessed their last gasp and they know it. Once the resistance makes some ground, there will be a general uprising. You agree, Rox?"

"Yeah. The people are cowed through fear but as soon as they stop being afraid, the regime will collapse. It's only a matter of when. The thing is, you can't kill the spirit that stirs up people to freedom."

"Guess not," smiled Alice. "Reassuring, but I don't want to die. Darth Vader Padget will probably have killed us *before* he gets done in, captured or whatever. Luke Skywalker is not out there tracking *us* in his X-wing."

"And I don't want anyone messing with my brain – even if it don't get them nowhere," stated Nadia, ruefully.

They fell silent, then Alice volunteered: "I know I was joking about Luke Skywalker but, you know, people *must* have missed us by now. I mean, we've been gone for ages. My parents would be looking for me for sure. *Someone* could be out there. We're not bound to—"

A key turned in the lock and the door swung open. A man stood in the doorway with a nasty looking gun and told them to stand against the far side of the cabin. A second man then entered with a tray with glasses of lemonade. He placed it on the floor. Then a third came in with a second tray bearing plates heaped with food. Finally, they retreated without a word and slammed and locked the door.

"Well, we ain't meant to die, like, just yet, it seems," chirped Nadia, her eyes bulging at the sight of food.

"Could be poisoned," suggested Alice.

"I don't care," said Nadia. "Let me at it."

Hen reassured them. "It won't be poisoned. They've got to keep us alive until we get to wherever we're going and the prof is fit enough to operate. If they want to dispose of us, all they have to do is chuck us overboard."

"Walk the plank?" Alice half joked.

"Nah," answered Tom. "They lack all semblance of romance. Goes with the territory. Sorry to say it, but when they've done with us, they'll just dump our bodies somewhere where no one will find them."

Roxanne picked up a chicken leg and made light of their situation as best she could. "Might as well enjoy the time we've got left, then."

Alice smiled. "You know what? I've got this feeling that we're going to survive this. I don't know why, but I have."

"Logic would dictate," stated Hen, "that the longer it goes before they get round to finishing us off, the more the odds swing in our favour."

"Right," said Tom. "So what do you reckon the odds are at

the moment, Hen?"

"Right now? There's no way of telling. But, say, if it was ten per cent this morning, by this afternoon it'll be fifteen... possibly."

"As low as that!" exclaimed Alice. "Rubbish! I would put it at at least seventy-five per cent in our favour."

"And where's your logic?" asked Hen.

"She ain't got none!" retorted Nadia. "Have you, Alice? It's just a gut feeling. And gut feelings matter. They come from..." She threw her arms out. She didn't rightly know where they came from.

"God?" suggested Tom.

Nadia shrugged again. "Yeah, I guess. Could do. Why not? What do you reckon, Alice?"

"Yeah, well, maybe." Alice wasn't sure how you could know God was or wasn't there.

"So, if God's with us, that narrows the odds even more, don't it?" concluded Nadia.

"Yes," said Hen. "That's logical."

Nadia was impatient. "So why don't you say a prayer over this food, Rox? Go for it, or else there won't be any food left to pray about."

Rox thanked God for the food.

"Amen... Yeah, God," declared Nadia and added, "And just you mind you look after my head, while you're at it!"

18

McBlair was shocked when she saw two blue and yellow police cars pull into the drive of the castle followed by the DI in his black saloon. She met the officers at the door.

"What's wrong, Inspector? Why all these cars?"

"Where are they?" he asked, curtly.

"Who, inspector?" McBlair was all innocence.

"Don't play with me. You know who. I want to know what you have done with the young people the Met are looking for. They have been here and I want to know where they are now."

"I really can't help you, inspector. Like I told you, they were taken away," she said as sweetly as she knew how. "I really had no idea—"

"What can you tell me about a red Toyota van?"

"A red van? I can't say—"

"Sergeant," instructed the DI, ignoring her protestations, "we're looking for a red Toyota van or any clue as to where the youngsters may have been taken to. Check the outbuildings."

"You can't just—" began McBlair.

"Oh, yes, we can. Where we know persons to be in immediate danger, we are empowered to mount a search. The teenagers were collected and brought here in the back of a red Toyota van. An unusual form of transport for people, wouldn't you say?"

Audra McBlair continued in her protest – now with a hint of defiance in her voice. "It may have been a red van. I didn't take much notice. Forms of transport aren't my thing."

The inspector's phone bleeped. He checked to see that it was coming from his HQ. It was. He answered it. "Good," he responded. "Get forensics on to it..."

Turning to McBlair, he said. "So they've found the red van. The driver is in custody. He appears to be one of your employees sent to dispose of it. Now he's looking after his own interests and telling all, I suggest you do the same, Miss McBlair."

"Are you arresting me, inspector?"

"That will depend on how much you are prepared to tell me and how much lying you do. What does Donald Padget do when he is here? And don't tell me he comes just for the sport. We see him in the closed season as well."

☆☆☆

The van had been illegally parked in Glasgow but the driver had been spotted as he had made to walk away and told to move it. He had, but not very far – he was too anxious to be careful. The police were called when he left it at a bus stop and they were already tracking him on CCTV when the call for the red van had gone out. They caught up with him at the railway station and arrested him.

Frightened more by the police than by what might happen to him at Inverlochie, he confirmed he had transported five teenagers. The police were closing in. This had gone beyond a search for five missing young people – what was emerging was Padget's involvement in something the international security network was only just beginning to become aware of. Exactly how big a threat it was, was not yet known but significant alarm bells were ringing in the security services of both the UK and USA.

Audra McBlair, unaware of what the police already knew, was doing her best to continue to paint a picture of an innocuous American who owned a Scottish estate for the fun of it.

"But, Inspector," she protested, now seated in her office, "it is not unnatural for a rich American to want to own something so beautiful. You grew up in these parts?" she asked. The inspector made no reply. "Growing up here you probably take a lot of this for granted. But to an urban American, you cannot imagine the magical allure of the Highlands."

"Oh, I can. This place is remote but near the Atlantic coast, underpopulated and private, yet sufficiently on the tourist track to mean that anyone can come and go without raising suspicion. The ideal place to blend in without having to show your passport."

"I assure you, Inspector, Mr Padget always shows his passport. He usually arrives at Prestwick."

"Glad to hear it. What about other people?"

"What other people?"

"The people that occupy your rooms. Mr Padget's guests."

"Some are invited and brought here by Mr Padget himself. Others come because he wants to provide them with a bit of R and R."

"And who brought the young people here? Do you often have young people around the castle, Miss McBlair?"

"No. These were an exception. We were just helping out a farmer who wanted them off his land. We're not really geared for youth. I've no idea how they got here."

"Which is why they left so quickly?"

"I've really no idea, Inspector. They were not ours. They were collected and left. That's all I know."

The sergeant reappeared. "Excuse me, sir. I think you may be interested in this."

"Remain here, Miss McBlair. I will be back."

"Would you and your men like tea, inspector?"

"Tempting as the offer is, I think I shall have to decline this time." He stood up and stepped out of the door with his colleague, leaving Audra McBlair looking decidedly uncomfortable. "What is it, Sergeant?"

"We've found old clothes. They might be the ones we're looking for - five sets, two male and three female, old fashioned and muddy."

"So," said the DI, pleased. "They haven't been destroyed. They fit the description given by the farmer. Have them sent to forensics. I want them matched to the DNA from London. And it might give us a clue to the identity of the extra girl."

"And, sir. We also found this in the bin." The sergeant produced the remains of a mobile phone. "Could this have belonged to one of them? I know teenagers are not noted for being careful with phones."

The inspector squinted at the remains of Padget's mobile as it lay in the sergeant's gloved hand. "Expensive bit of kit. I doubt this belonged to a young person - unless he or she has particularly well-off parents. It's the latest top of the range, I believe."

"The sort that catches fire in people's pockets?" joked the sergeant.

"I think they've got that sorted these days," smiled the inspector. "In any case, this hasn't caught fire. Just got rather badly damaged. More than just dropped, I would say... more likely deliberately smashed. This could be important. Get it to forensics, too, immediately. Well done."

"Of course, sir. Thank you, sir."

The inspector's phone rang again. "Ullapool?" he said. "That's interesting. So our red van gets around a bit... yes... yes. It might be connected. Keep me posted... So our red van has turned up in Glasgow but not before being spotted in Ullapool," he reported.

"Ullapool?" said the sergeant. "The coastguard is searching for the owner of a scalloper there that was found drifting quite a way out, I heard."

"So I believe," concurred the DI.

"It was reported missing; it didn't return before nightfall as expected. Apparently – according to the skipper's family – he was commissioned to take a small party on a private fishing trip. Life belts and a raft are missing but so far they haven't found anyone in the area."

"That's what I heard," confirmed the inspector. "I want the two investigations connected. It's not often that two mysterious incidents happen in a small place like Ullapool on the same day."

19

Padget's new phone bleeped his messages. He was in a modest suite belonging to the Hôtel Shangri-La in Paris. After leaving Inverlochie Castle, he had decided to put an international boundary between himself and any inquisitive intrusions. Arriving at Prestwick he had bought a seat on the first available flight to another country. It turned out to be France and so now he was slumming it in Parisian luxury.

He noted a text message from McBlair with some concern but it seemed she was doing a good job. She had ordered the van to be taken to Glasgow and the driver to get the train back to London where the van was registered and then report it stolen. He did not know the driver had not got even as far as Glasgow Central.

Padget sighed. These disturbed brats were proving more trouble than they were worth. But he could not go back on the plan now. He had too much invested in Williams, and not just money. He would lose face and power with the other members of the Daisychain, and he did not want that. He knew they were all people as ruthless, if not more so than he was. And anyway, the kids knew too much – they had to be kept away from the authorities.

Padget relaxed. He had every reason to believe the five were already on their way to the Daisychain's headquarters near Ålesund in Norway. Although it appeared from the front to be a simple secure warehouse for storing valuables, the remote building had a command base constructed in the hillside behind. This facility boasted a secret laboratory – a laboratory recently fitted out with the equipment ordered by Prof W. No one would ever find the young people there.

20

DI Renshaw drew up at the Winterford clinic. He had news – they were at last on the trail of the young people and, so far, the news was good; although they hadn't yet found them, they had turned up in Scotland. They were all alive.

Tom's mother wept uncontrollably – she hadn't slept at all since she had arrived. Nadia's dad was not taking in much. Alice's parents let out sighs of huge relief as they clung to each other.

The inspected explained. "They were seen by a Scottish farmer and taken away in a red van belonging to a Scottish country estate."

Mrs Brean took in a sharp breath.

"You know the estate I'm referring to, Mrs Brean?"

The housekeeper nodded.

"Along the way," continued Renshaw, "our four young people seem to have collected a fifth person, a girl whom the Scottish farmer described as white with brown hair." Mrs Brean started again. DI Renshaw took her aside.

"Have you an idea who this girl might be, Mrs Brean?"

"There was a girl here called Roxanne Battie. She left – very suddenly. Nadia Simpson was already here when Roxanne left. Professor Williams was quite upset about her going. I never heard where she went. I came in one morning and she was gone. She left most of her things in her room. I found that strange but the professor thought she may intend to return and asked me to pack them and store them."

"Was there anything among them that we could use to test for DNA – a hairbrush, for example?"

"I think so. Her stuff is in the store room. I'll get it."

The DI ordered Roxanne's belongings to be transferred to the police station.

Mrs Brean found Roxanne's file in the filing cabinet. It appeared that she had been in a children's home and then fostered from being a baby. There was no record of her birth mother.

The inspector ordered someone to go to the last foster home – an address in Romford – and get all the information they could furnish.

Hen's uncle began asking more questions. What condition were the young people reported to be in? Were they safe?

"As I understand it," stated the inspector, "they turned up at a place called Inverlochie. We have been investigating it – I think Mrs Brean can tell you about this place, can't you, madam? As far as we know they were all fine when they arrived there, but they are no longer there and we do not know their current whereabouts."

Tom's mother's anguish boiled over into anger. "What the hell are your people doing up there?" she demanded. "How come they found them and then lost them again?"

"I am sure the Scottish police are doing all they can," said Hen's uncle, in an attempt to calm her.

"It sounds pretty incompetent to me!" exclaimed Mrs. Green. "If anything happens to my son, your lot won't hear the last of it, I can tell you!"

"As I understand it, we haven't lost them, as you put it," explained Renshaw, defending his Scottish colleagues. "They were never in police hands. And I am sure that everything is being done to follow the trail... And when I say everything, I mean it," affirmed the DI, now with a sense of aplomb. "This is no longer simply a matter for the police – although you can be assured we will not be stinting in our efforts – it also involves the coastguard... and MI5."

"MI5!" exclaimed Rowena. "The British secret service? Like our CIA?"

"Not quite. That'll be MI6. MI5 is counter-intelligence; it deals with inland security."

"Isn't that the same as counter-terrorism?!" exclaimed Hen's uncle. "That sounds ominous. What have the kids got themselves mixed up in?"

The inspector cleared his throat and became very serious. "The nature of the MI5 investigation is, of course, classified but suffice it to say that when MI5 are involved, you can bet it's bigger than just four – or five – missing persons... and you can be absolutely confident that all the stops are being pulled out. Finding your children, ladies and gentlemen, is now a matter of national security."

21

Audra McBlair protested. "On what grounds am I being arrested? I have answered all your questions. All I do is the day-to-day management of this estate. I demand to be allowed to talk to the laird."

"I have already explained," repeated the inspector, "you are being arrested on suspicion of activities endangering the security of the realm. I'm afraid you will not be permitted to communicate with anyone for the time being."

"Preposterous. I demand a lawyer."

"That will be accorded you, Miss McBlair – if that is your real name. Sergeant, will you escort this lady to the station and see that she is formally charged?"

McBlair uttered a sound of disgust. "You are making a big mistake," she seethed, reaching for her bag.

"No miss, the officer will take that."

The look that Audra McBlair gave the DI was a mixture of loathing and defiance. He wondered what had happened to the sweet lady who had only an hour or so before offered him tea in the most polite manner. He shuddered. He had no idea what they had stumbled across but it was big. MI5 had arrived in numbers and were swarming all over Ullapool and his own division. He had intended to go down to Ullapool and see what the coastguard could tell him, but his chief constable had told him just to bring in McBlair and leave the rest to others.

22

In the port of Ullapool, the wife of Robbie McRae, the skipper of the *Miss of the Isles*, sat in her front room surrounded by her family in the way that the families of fishermen had done for centuries. In the past, herring and, later, mackerel had been the main catch; these days, it was nephrops and scallops.

But this time it was different because her husband hadn't been out trawling for the things that had kept him in business for the past twenty years; this time the *Miss of the Isles* had been hired by someone – she did not know the details – and her husband hadn't taken anyone else with him. He had reckoned on having an easy day. He had told her he thought he would be back for tea, long before dark. But now this was the third day and the coastguard had found no sign of him or anyone else, despite intensive searches. It seemed certain that since his boat turned up intact but abandoned, it was just a matter of time before the bodies were found.

And now MI5 had arrived and they were going over the boat with a fine tooth comb for the third time – her Robbie had got himself caught up in something much bigger than he could have ever thought possible.

Mary McRae sat in silence, drinking tea and waiting.

Then she looked up as they heard a gentle knock on the door - a dreaded knock. She always imagined that a gentle knock would mean bad news.

Her cousin stood to open the door and admit the harbour master. He stood just inside the front room; he wore a solemn expression and shook his head.

"They've found one of *Miss's* life rafts up the coast - Achduart. It must have gone overboard much nearer than the reported encounter with the boat near Mellon Udrigle. Could be nothing... No sign of anyone and no other debris."

He was offered a seat and he sat saying nothing more. Someone put a cup of tea into his hand and held out the sugar basin. He heaped spoonfuls into his cup - forgetting he didn't take sugar. There are no words to describe the way a person feels when a loved one is missing in tragic circumstances.

He reported that the results of the forensic investigations of the *Miss of the Isles* were what they were expecting. The boat had definitely been used to transport five missing young people. They had been taken to the port in a red van and transferred to the hold. The skipper probably would not have been allowed to return to tell the tale; whether he had been taken alive or killed was something they could not know. The fact that no bodies had been so far found, however, was positive news.

The fisherman's wife hardly heard the brighter news. The sedatives which the doctor had prescribed had prevented her from taking in much. Her sister sat beside her.

"There is hope," she assured. "If he's been taken captive, he's got plenty of bottle. He'll be looking after those young people you can bet."

"Let's hope so," murmured a minister from the Church of Scotland who was also among the people crowded into the small room. "Wherever he is, God has him in His hands."

"It doesn't feel like that!" spoke the sister on the verge of anger.

The minister took the blow. "I know. It doesn't... but that doesn't make it any less true," he said, softly. "God cares. He is hurting too."

Everyone fell silent. Words were not needed; there wasn't anything useful to be said.

☆☆☆

In London, the families of the young people were clinging on to the same hope. Mrs Brean glanced towards the bottom drawer of her boss's filing cabinet and thought of him in the clutches of that awful Donald Padget. She was utterly convinced he, too, was a victim of Padget's game – he had been a pawn for months. If only the professor had managed to find the elusive evidence and complete his paper; what a wonderful, glorious moment that would have been. But Padget had taken advantage of the financial situation and was, it seemed, in it for far more than commercial interests. Who would have thought?

23

On board the big white yacht, the young people polished their plates. They really had been very hungry.

After the meal, they had had a chance to visit a small bathroom at the end of the corridor and clean up a bit before the key had been turned in the door of the cabin once more. Now the need to sleep was overtaking them. They selected a bunk each and just lay on it as they were, and slept.

They did not know how long they had been sleeping when the door opened and a rough voice ordered the girls out. There was nothing they could do.

Terrified, they followed the crewman along the corridor to the bathroom where he issued them with a soft towel each and a posh summer-weight dress. "The captain says that that is all he has if you choose to wear them. You are expected to be clean on board this vessel." He spoke in a foreign-sounding voice with a strange lilt that Alice couldn't identify.

"Where are we headed?" asked Alice.

"All in good time. Now wash."

A few anxious minutes later the girls returned looking like

celebrities in upper-class designer dresses. The boys breathed a sigh of relief – they had spent a quarter of an hour wondering what hell their friends were being put through.

"Not so bad, then?" smiled Tom, as lightly as he could.

"No comments on the gear, please," sneered Nadia. "No choice. Apparently, we're 'all expected to be clean on board this vessel'," she said with the imitation of a posh-sounding voice and striking a pose that made Hen laugh.

The crew member beckoned to the boys. "Now you."

"About time!" mocked Nadia. "If you want your girlfriend to love you, Tom, you'd better do somut about the smell."

Alice pretended not to hear. She was embarrassed by her new dress which was too low-cut and too short for her liking, although on this occasion – unlike at the farm – it fitted her.

The bathroom had a porthole through which Tom peered. All he could see was the ocean but it was possible to ascertain that the ship was no slouch. "We're making good headway," he said. "I wouldn't like to put a figure on it, but we're doing a fair amount of knots."

"Which direction?" asked Hen.

"Dunno. Can't tell. There's no sun; it's overcast. And I can see no land... I doubt they'll head south into the Irish Sea, though."

"Get on with it," ordered the man with the foreign voice as gruffly as he was able. "There's nothing but sea to see out there."

"But I like the sea," answered Tom. "It's pretty calm at the moment."

"When it gets rough, you'll know."

"So where are you taking us?" asked Hen.

"You're as bad as the girls. All talk and questions... Get washed. Here are your clothes."

Tom was not as lucky as Alice – the shorts didn't fit and the stripy tea-shirt really made everyone snicker. Being fed and washed, however, no matter what their circumstances, was bound to lift morale. And now that they understood that they were to be taken somewhere, and nothing bad was likely to befall them while they were at sea, they relaxed a little.

The hours passed and the food kept coming. There really was nothing they could do until the yacht got into port or they were taken ashore; they had no way of taking over a large vessel.

The five young people were not aware that as they drew near to their destination, the Daisychain had devised a way of transferring them that, once again, required them to be asleep.

24

As she slipped from consciousness, Roxanne reached out for her friends. The last thing she was aware of was a look of concern and then fear on Hen's face as he held her.

Suddenly and unexpectedly, there sprang up a surge of life from within her. She was inside the fifth but not as she had known it before. She was drifting peacefully but slowly sinking through the slope. She heard a voice, low and soft but firm. It sounded familiar but she could not give a name to the one who spoke.

"Come, Roxanne, named for the dawn – the rising of the sun to a fresh new day – come, die with me awhile. Let me take you. Do not be alarmed." She looked up and saw the face of a mother. Her mother? She had never known her mother. But now she was sure she was in the presence of her true mother in whom she had been conceived and created.

She resisted for a second and then relaxed as she sank completely through the grey plane into a deep pink and red world in which she knew she was wonderfully loved. She was surrounded on all sides with a love that was perfectly pure, untarnished, unblemished by any false motive or emotion.

"Love?" she gasped. "I am loved?"

"You always have been, Roxanne, daughter of the new day, from the moment of your conception. You always will be unto eternity."

"But I have never known love. Not true love," she protested. "I was never wanted. My father wasn't interested. My mother rejected me. I am an orphan of the state. No one would risk their life for me as they would their own. Love is a mystery – something others speak of."

"And yet, Roxanne, you are mine and always will be. I have loved you from the beginning. How else would you recognise love in all its fullness? Roxanne, I call you by name."

Roxanne sank as if into the softest bed; strength and belief coursed through her veins. "I am loved!" she declared.

"I have called you by name – you are mine! This eternity is yours but the time is not yet. Now sleep, my child, until it is beholden on you to return."

Hen held Roxanne and watched as she slid from consciousness. Had she been drugged? There had been nothing in the food before. This time it must have been there; he became certain as he felt his own mind grow hazy. His last thought before slumping over the still form of Roxanne was that he should resist this with all his might – but he could not. It was as if he had flipped but he had no control; he had no power within it and he felt himself being sucked beneath the forty-five-degree plane.

"Come, Christopher," he heard, "Come, you who are named for the bearer of Christ – kind, generous and caring. Come Christopher and die with me awhile. Fear not." There before him, stood a figure like Bertrand Russell, or was it Einstein or perhaps even Aristotle, himself?

The grey of the fifth gave way to a rich golden yellow. Here were fine structures – towers, arches and pyramids. Hen recognised the lattices of quantum power – electromagnetic energy, in which each particle and wave knew where it belonged. Somehow, he understood that the uncertainty principle applied merely to human scientists who could not see the universe in all its fullness. But here, at that moment, Hen saw and marvelled at the perfection of order and symmetry before him.

Exactly how Hen knew this, he could not tell but he was surrounded by a mathematical completeness that extended into infinity – unto eternity.

"How can this be?" he marvelled. "How can I witness this? I am a mere human being."

"Human, yes. And as such, you have a unique gift of understanding. There is nothing 'mere' about being human.

You, Christopher, are precious," spoke the scientist. "You are a person who has been entrusted with the power of knowledge and discovery. Behold, before you the eternity to explore, wave upon wave, particle upon particle of pure joy that will enable you to grow and become, and continue to become, forever."

Hen felt completely fulfilled. If this was death, let it continue! "Thank you. I shall begin!"

"But, no, Christopher, bearer and carer, now is not the time. Your friends need you. I have called you by name – you are mine. But rest now before it is time for you the return."

Alice knew she should not have eaten the food. They had been too cocky. Rox had gone quiet and Hen was looking concerned. Nadia, despite her brown skin, was looking pale, too. "Tom," she called. "Don't ... I ... Tom!" But as she reached for him she found herself inside the fifth. Yet this time, the plane was not supporting her weight – she was sinking through it. It was as if she was in a highland bog all over again. Where was Tom to drag her back? Was this it? – forever?!

Alice determined that her final thoughts were not going to be ones of terror but of being held... and kissed. And it was granted her.

"Come, Alice," a light gentle voice called to her, "Come,

noble one. As your name declares you, you are indeed noble and upright. Come and die with me awhile. Do not be frightened."

The speaker was her former headteacher, Mr Oakland. She had always admired him – he knew all his students by name, even though there must have been thousands of them over the years. And now, here he was inside the fifth calling her by name again.

Alice opened her eyes and saw that the grey had given way to greens of every hue – vibrant, soft, light and rich velvet. The place smelt like a forest – clean and fresh.

Alice sensed the power of it before she realised what surrounded her – Truth. Honest, perfect and unmitigated truth permeated every living green thing. Here, there was no deception, no lie – here was reality true to itself in all its fullness... and Alice felt foul. She was bad and rotten – a conniving hussy – and she wanted to hide; the shame was so powerful.

"Don't be scared," Mr Oakland said again. "You are seeing this because you value and know the truth more than any of them. You, noble one, can look upon pure Truth and live. Remain true unto eternity and you will rejoice as you never thought possible. Alice, you have the power to live the whole truth. All that is not true in you has been washed away. You are forgiven because you long for it with a true heart. You are well named, Alice, noble daughter of the Creator."

Alice marvelled. She felt her own forgiven soul fill with the fresh green of Truth and was truly happy.

Yet Mr Oakland turned to her and said, "But your time here is not yet, Alice. You must go back, noble one, and bring blessings and freedom on those given you to love and care for. Best rest a while before your return."

Tom watched the room swim. The fifth had come upon him as quickly as the first time on the quayside. But inside, it was not the same. It was odd; the grey plane was not right. Tom felt as if... was he... dying?

The grey plane refused to bear him as it always had done before and Tom plunged through like diving through the waves of the sea – like his father must have done the day he had died when the *Merry Linch* had foundered.

"Oh, Tom, be not afraid. Do not doubt but trust me. Come, die with me awhile."

Tom knew that his name – Thomas – was the same as the disciple of Jesus who had doubted his Lord's resurrection. Tom had not seen himself as a boy who doubted things more than anyone else in his generation. Yet he lacked trust, as they all did.

But what was all this about? Was he dying? Was he dead?

"Tom," called the voice again. Tom looked up and all was blue. There was the blue of the sky and the blue of the sea, separated only by tall pure white cliffs and the white surf below them. It was not at all threatening.

The sky was filled with the sound of blue birds soaring on the thermals and he heard the strains of Vera Lynn singing, "There'll be bluebirds over the white cliffs of Dover" – a song his mother loved because it reminded her of her father, Tom's grandpappi, who had made his bid for freedom across the Channel – a flight from the evil tyranny of the Nazis.

"Tom!" he heard once more. And there he was: Pappi.

In that moment, Tom became aware of sheer goodness. In this blue world, there was nothing bad or evil. Those things lay beyond – out of sight. Here, there was only light and no darkness at all. Tom was surrounded by pure Goodness.

"Yes, Tom." His pappi smiled. "Goodness is forever. Nothing bad can last long; evil gets caught up by the powerful waves of goodness and is overcome – as darkness vanishes in the light. Son, I have come to you to give you courage. Sometimes the darkness will seem to win, but don't be afraid, it will not – it cannot. Remember you were created wholly good and to Goodness you shall return."

"But how can I be good all the time?" protested Tom. "I try

hard but I fail."

Pappi smiled. "Do not doubt, Tom. Trust. Remember that the goodness does not spring from you alone but from the One that is good unto eternity. No fleeting earthly darkness can conquer the Light."

The birds sang and Tom relaxed as he absorbed the pure goodness of the blue world.

"Tom," called his pappi. "You have to return soon. You cannot remain here now; you have goodness to share and you have friends to love and care for. You must go back to them. They need you. Yet rest a while longer before you go."

Tom fell into a deep sleep, basking in the gentle warm wind of freedom.

Nadia swore. They had got her. She knew it. Why had she eaten that stuff? She must not pass out! She watched Hen catch hold of Roxanne and then drift off himself.

They ain't getting my brain! Nadia tried to yell it out loud but it wouldn't come. She attempted to stand but her legs wouldn't work. Finally, she summed up as much power as she could to get into the fifth where they wouldn't find her.

To her amazement, Nadia did enter the grey world; she was free! She tried to climb but the grey plane soon became sticky and she began to sink beneath the surface and she grew afraid. Was she going to die?

"Oh, God." she called, "I didn't mean to be rude. Honest!"

"I am not offended." A powerful voice filled her consciousness. "You say it as you mean it. Blunt is fine because your heart is beautiful."

"What! Hey, are you God? Where are you? And in case you hadn't noticed, I ain't beautiful."

The grey fifth had given way to every colour of the spectrum. There was a rainbow beneath her feet and a huge rainbow spanned the sky above.

"I am within you and around you," spoke the voice. "I know your heart. Come die with me awhile and I will show you."

"That's, like, scary, innit?!"

"You need have no fear. I am Light, I live and your life is upheld by mine. I created you."

Nadia blinked but the rainbows were still there. The whole place was astonishingly beautiful.

"Nadia, I have called you by name. Do you not know what your name means?"

"Nah. It's Russian, innit?"

"Indeed. In Russian, it means 'hope'. You are to hope and be a blessing of hope in dull and sad places. I call you to light them with your beauty."

"I told you, I ain't beautiful!"

"Who are you, child, to argue with me? You are mine. I created you. You cannot but be full of perfect beauty – unless you choose to destroy it."

"How can I do that?"

"By trying to be all the things you are not, Nadia. You are neither selfish nor unkind; you do not lie. You love your father as I do, even though his afflictions render him trying and difficult."

"Yeah. Well..."

"Accept it, Nadia! You are beautiful – not as the narrow world may judge but, as you live and breathe in me and I in you, you are made perfectly beautiful."

"OK. You're the boss... I guess, like, I've snuffed it. So is this world of rainbows where I am to live forever?"

"It is, and there are infinitely more beautiful things to discover. But not yet, Nadia, child of hope. You must return to your friends and bless them with your beauty and your frankness. Bring them nadia – hope. You promised them, 'All for one and one for all!' You remember?"

"Yeah."

"I call you by name, oh, girl of hope. You are mine. Go when you are bid. Bring them rainbows! In the meantime, you may rest a while and absorb the beauty of your Creator."

25

At dawn in the United States – the upmarket end of Arlington, Virginia, to be precise – the FBI had descended in force on Donald Padget's sleeping family. His wife, three teenage daughters and his mother, who was sleeping over that night, were awakened by the crash of the front door and then surprised by armed men storming into their bedrooms. The eighteen-year-old, Daisy, who was not totally ignorant of her father's long-term plans, wondered if the war had begun. Was the world takeover underway?

"It's OK," she heard herself say. "We're on your side."

"You bet you are," growled the agent. He pulled a housecoat from the back of the door. "Make yourself decent and get downstairs."

Instinctively, she reached for her cell phone – as any eighteen-year-old would. The phone had become part of her; without it, she felt distinctly underdressed.

"Sorry, miss. No phones."

"What? What's going on?"

"Explanations downstairs."

In the hallway, another agent directed her into the large lounge. As she went, she noticed the wreck of the front door that the FBI had burst open.

"What—?"

She saw her mother on the far side of the room being questioned about the whereabouts of her husband.

"What is this all about?" asked the eighteen-your-old, in as strident a voice as she could muster. "I demand—"

"No lady. We ask the questions. Where's Donald Padget?"

Mrs Padget, still in shock, strove to speak. "He... He left three days ago for his castle in Scotland... He... He has business interests in the UK."

"When do you expect him to return, ma'am?"

"That I cannot say. I don't know."

"When did he last call you?"

"Yesterday."

"Where did he say he was?"

"He didn't," replied Mrs Padget, exasperation mixed with the confusion and astonishment. "I assumed he was in Scotland. He didn't talk long, he was busy,"

"Why did he call?"

"Why does any husband call his wife and family?" she

protested.

"Nothing more?"

"Look, I really don't understand what all this is about." She slumped into a chair.

Padget's daughter directed looks of contempt at the man guarding her. She had a pretty good idea what this was about – her father had goofed up.

In Paris, for want of nothing better to do, Donald Padget wandered down the Champs-Elysées pushing his way through the masses of American tourists popping in and out of the shops and creating noisy huddles in the pavement cafés. The Frenchness of the place seemed almost – but not quite – lost under the pressure of American English. The *pains au chocolat* and *croissants* had not yet been displaced by bagels, but the French eateries were battling against a tide of Italian pizzerias and Chinese restaurants in the capital's side streets. Padget sank into a chair under the canopy of a small establishment off the main boulevard and was almost immediately approached by a waiter. "*Menu, monsieur?*"

"*S'il vous plaît.*" What the hell, he might as well enjoy himself while he was here.

Padget attacked a *crôque-monsieur* with care. He hadn't intended to come to Paris. This was the first time he had ever taken a plane without a preconceived plan. He did have a plan now, of course. It consisted of laying low until he deemed the clouds had cleared and the questions had ceased.

Donald Padget sincerely regretted being caught up in the Professor Williams thing. At first, he thought the problem was only about money, but of late he had begun to wonder whether the man was a charlatan - not a deliberate liar exactly but a man who had lost the plot and was never going to deliver. And then, if only he had not tried to appease his subjects and shown them so much of the outside world. They had become too sure of themselves and outwitted him. The last time had been too close for comfort; it had only been down to a stroke of luck - luck he could not explain - that they had got the teenagers back at all.

Padget took out his new phone and checked it. The amazing thing was that, apart from the one text, he had heard nothing from anyone in Scotland. The phone was working though - he had got through to his home in Arlington without any difficulty. He toyed with phoning or, at least, texting. But if they were onto Inverlochie... No, surely not? But he needed to know what was happening.

He was on the point of trying when the phone bleeped. A text; it was excellent news. The message was from Ålesund centre. It simply read: "The package has arrived in good shape." Padget relaxed and smiled as he chased his crôque-monsieur with a good red wine and a dessert of crêpes filled with a mixture of blueberries and raspberries dusted with icing sugar. *There are worse places to lie low,* he reflected. The "package" had arrived and he had had no other adverse news. He'd give it a few more days and then return home to Arlington. Life was good again.

26

A large white private yacht arrived in the port of Ålesund, Norway. It delivered five slim crates, two metres long and two metres high and marked with arrows indicating that they had be kept upright. They were addressed to the warehouse facility located on a nearby island covered in trees. The crates contained framed paintings; the pictures were old but not particularly valuable.

Nevertheless, the customs authorities checked every consignment for the warehouse to see that the contents of each crate were consistent with its accompanying paperwork.

Officers opened the tops of the upright crates and verified the number of carefully packed paintings; everything appeared to be above-board. The crates were then resealed and loaded onto a lorry to be taken to the warehouse.

What the customs authorities did not know was that at the bottom of each of the crates under a false floor was an unconscious drugged young person. Nor were they aware at that time that an innocuous-looking fishing boat making its way past a huge cruise ship moored on the quayside, had an

English professor on board.

☆ ☆ ☆

Unbeknown to Donald Padget, in a laboratory in Glasgow, forensic hardware engineers had managed to repair his former phone. Despite all appearances, the damage was not fatal and they soon had it working – and in even less time had hacked into it to research its memory.

It had clearly belonged to Padget. The contacts he had made in the past six months were all revealed. There were calls to his family in Arlington and numbers in other parts of the States and London – including the Winterford – and new, as yet unknown contacts in other parts of the world, too. An interesting number in Norway featured remarkably often.

The final picture in the phone's memory depicted five young people with dark defiant expressions on their faces. They were dressed in the outlandish clothes they had retrieved at the castle – so it had clearly been taken on the evening of their recapture. It was proof that Donald Padget had not only known about them but had also been there himself; or, at least, his phone had.

MI5 was checking out all the numbers. One of them in London was a man who had been on their watch list for some time before being arrested along with others for threatening behaviour outside a mosque the previous year.

His flat had turned out to be covered in swastikas and anti-Semitic and Islamophobic graffiti, but he had not been imprisoned. Could these other numbers have among them contacts of right-wing activists? MI5 shared this intelligence with the FBI. The Norwegian number was forwarded to the Norwegian Intelligence Service - *E-tjenesten*.

Since the Norway attack on 22nd July 2011, the Norwegian government had been alert to the threat in their country of right-wing extremists, and the intelligence from MI5 triggered an immediate response.

The Norwegian authorities identified the phone number as belonging to a senior employee at the storage facility near Ålesund and investigated it.

It was unusual that the warehouse appeared to be staffed by people living on-site and had little to do with anyone in the local area. Local tradesmen: plumbers, electricians and carpenters were never called upon. And quite why so many people from different parts of the world wanted to store their things at this particular warehouse was also strange. A great deal of attention was being paid to this innocuous-looking white-painted building.

27

Having been met at the quayside, Professor Williams was in a sombre mood. He had almost recovered from his encounter with the Scottish seas but continued to make out he was sick and weak. It wasn't difficult. He knew he owed his life to the young people's care. He also knew that it was because of their concern for him and Wood that they had been so easily re-apprehended. Their pursuers had used him as bait. He told himself he should have warned them, but he had not been fully aware or fully himself. He kept hearing Nadia saying, "Course." It was so natural for her to care – it didn't appear to have occurred to her to put her safety before his welfare. He was also impressed by the way the five worked together.

Williams noted the beauty of the fjord. Sweet-scented pine and birch lined the road as they passed the last of the low wooden houses beside the deep narrow inlets surrounded by round-topped hills. The air felt clean and fresh against his face. There was something about just being alive that was good; something less easily understood in the hurly-burly of London and the clinical nature of the scientific laboratory. *I have been missing something,* he thought, as the car crossed a bridge and a magnificent view of the fjord was revealed. *Have these youngsters understood something about life that I have been failing to see for decades?* They continued east beside a calm long lake dotted with water birds, then turned north and crossed a small inlet before climbing towards the fjords and islands beyond. Finally, they approached a modern white warehouse, gleaming in the low Norwegian sun. It was set with its back against a steep wooded slope.

Inside the facility were the things the professor needed to perform his final and conclusive investigation. Part of him was still sure he would succeed in surgically identifying the site of the neurological centre that induced the fifth dimension experiences – his own faith in his research had never dimmed; he had little respect for the line that Professor Bradford was taking in the US. He was sure he was right and if he had proved himself such and stood to receive his prize, he would have been the hero of the world.

But now it would never be like that. At least not for him. All his valuable research was going to be used for the cause of a right-wing movement with dubious credentials. Oh yes, he may become the darling of the new order that he had been hearing about so passionately on board the yacht. A few years from now, he was told, the White House, the Kremlin, the Chinese party-machine and everywhere else that mattered would all be under the ownership of this new movement. There were British political figures lined up to occupy Downing Street and the royal family would be carefully removed with outward dignity but efficient ruthlessness. Prof W had been both shocked and impressed at the depth of the movement.

And now here he was, approaching one of their secret headquarters. Taking in the stunning views, he reflected that he had finally arrived in Scandinavia but not to receive a Nobel prize - not in its present form at any rate. Who knew what would follow in a new world order ushered in by the Daisychain movement?

Professor Williams was acutely aware that he had a choice to make that was no longer about glory, fame and financial security but whether or not he would leave this place alive at all.

As the car drew up outside the warehouse, he had no idea his arrival was being monitored on the screens of the Norwegian Intelligence Service. From the forests high above the facility, two NIS agents were monitoring and videoing all the comings and goings and Prof W was recorded as he got out of the passenger seat of a silver Volvo V40.

Less than an hour later, in London, Mrs Brean was watching the footage. She confirmed that that was indeed her professor.

"You've found him! He's alive! What a relief. Where is he?"

"All in good time," assured DI Renshaw. "All in good time," he repeated, laying a hand on the agitated housekeeper's shoulder.

"What about the children?" she asked.

"I have no news of them, madam," said the inspector. "But I have a hunch that we are not far behind."

28

Once inside the warehouse, the professor couldn't help being impressed. Behind and beneath the storage rooms was a suite of offices and a strong room as well as accommodation and the medical suite. It was a proverbial TARDIS – the building had been extended back into the hillside. They passed a security suite with screens displaying the images of dozens of CCTV cameras arranged at strategic sites around the above-ground building. The place was staffed by an army of security guards – soldiers – in far greater numbers than anyone would ever guess from the outside.

At the heart of the complex was a spacious control room with screens and displays that ranged from an interactive map of the whole planet, through TV screens relaying satellite images from the world's media to communications consoles that monitored and controlled agents in all six continents. When the time came, the move against the world would be coordinated from this place.

Prof W became aware that he was a small but important cog in this empire. Control of the fifth dimension would give them a real edge. So far the world had been in virtual denial –

once the truth of the true existence and power of the fifth, and who knows how many more dimensions, was revealed, then more and more subjects would be forthcoming. When they could develop beyond mere identification and monitoring to being able to control and use the fifth it would be life-changing. It would transform the human potential.

Preparations for a technological coup were already well advanced. Computer hackers in bedrooms and college dorms were being groomed and recruited and would be used to trigger a simultaneous Internet takeover from multiple platforms. It was all centred here and when the time came, it would be from here that the command would be given and the attack launched. Not just one domino effect, but many.

Prof W was escorted through to the medical facilities suite. He noted the state-of-the-art scanners, quantum microscopes and electronic paraphernalia, and then the operating theatre equipped with the latest surgical instruments to enable him to investigate a living brain; this was heaven – or as near as you could get to heaven for a neuroscientist on earth. Professor Williams would no longer be a cranky scientist in his own small clinic, ignored by the world and in debt up to his eyeballs; he would be the master of all this. All he had to do was probe and then dissect the brains of five ordinary British teenagers – and, if he did it right, perhaps he would not need all of them.

In years to come, they themselves could become

celebrated – acknowledged as willing martyrs in the cause of science. Could he work with that? Within less than an hour, the first could be here in this theatre. She was already drugged – drugged as she had enjoyed a plate of luxury food unaware of what it contained. She would not need to regain consciousness until she was opened and wired up – until then she would know nothing of where she was and what was happening to her. It would be easy.

It should have been easy, but it wasn't. This girl was not just a subject with an ability for travelling into the fifth dimension, she had a name – Nadia – and was endowed with a unique personality. For all he knew, she was loved too – by a father who had signed the papers entrusting her to him for a cure. And this same Nadia had almost certainly saved his life.

In her naïvety, Nadia had shown him what goodness was. She knew what was right – for her, there had been no choice. "Course," he kept hearing her say. The question, now, was: had he her courage?

He had a choice. He could refuse to do this and take the inevitable consequences. That wouldn't save the young people – short of a miracle, nothing could now – but their deaths would not forward Daisychain's horrific designs.

But to walk away from all this state-of-the-art pristine machinery... with the possibility – no, probability – of being proved right and concluding his paper...

Professor Reginald Williams, MD, FRCS, SN brought himself back to the reality of the situation and resolved to pull himself together. He spoke with dry efficiency.

"Thank you. This looks all in order. But I need to test the equipment carefully. In order to perform the histological examination, I require slides of the highest standard. The microtome blade needs to be in perfect condition. Any bluntness or nicks will result in squishing or longitudinal tears. I also need to check you have all the dyes and chemicals necessary in preparing the specimen slides. Proper staining and mounting of the tissue are vital. Before I begin on the girl, I shall need other brain tissue on which to test all these things... an animal will do, any animal as long as it is freshly dead."

The chief looked at him, crossly.

"I have followed all your demands, professor. We have installed all the equipment to your precise specifications – all brought here in various ways so as not to raise suspicion, and now you tell me you don't trust it!"

"Oh. It's not that. I'm sure it is all exactly as it should be – you have done well. But in order for it to be of any use, it has to be tested and calibrated, that's all."

"How long will this take?"

"First, I need to sleep. I have not been through the easiest of times, lately; a few days ago I was near to death. Then, if you can find me a specimen tomorrow morning I will begin the testing. If all runs smoothly, within three days I could begin to tackle the subject..."

"That long?!"

"My man, this is the culmination of years of work. In order to produce the result, patience is required... Look, you wouldn't have your mother take a cake out of the oven ten minutes before it's ready. She's spent hours on sieving, blending, beating, lining the baking tin, preheating the oven and so on – taking it out of the oven just a little early will spoil the whole thing. No, my man. You need to be patient. The results will prove nothing if I do not perform them precisely. And I need the subjects to be kept alive and in pristine condition until I'm ready."

"You did not tell us you needed a custody suite!"

"How you keep them is up to you – but please, no more drugs – too much of that and their brains could be damaged and the results skewed. I want vibrant, healthy brain tissue... beginning with an animal in, say, ten hours from now. Now, please show me to my quarters."

Before turning in, Prof W asked to see the subject. He was conducted to a small room next to the lab and operating theatre. Nadia was laid on her back on a trolley with her head on a small pillow and her arms by her side. She still wore the fine sleeveless dress with which she had been issued. It finished a few inches above her knees. She had nothing on her feet. The professor looked at her. Lying there, she looked so perfect - beautiful even. The professor caught his breath as he heard her voice etched on his brain: "Course."

He had always thought that science was the most beautiful thing in the cosmos - its order, its symmetry, its complexity - everything so predictable and precise. People, as they were to be found in general society, were flawed and gross - ignorant for the most part of what they were really capable of.

Nadia was not cultured - her upbringing had been patchy and sparse. When she spoke with her lazy Bristolian accent it sounded like water running down a drain - all uncontrolled vowels and indistinct consonants - "Course ..." But when it came to exploring the final pieces of "the fifth" she was the perfect subject... She lay there ready to be injected with the exact combination of drugs in the precise doses that would cause no damage to the brain tissues, ready to be probed and tested even as she still lived.

Prof W shuddered. He suddenly became aware of a truth that had not preoccupied his scientific mind much: Human beings are more than the sum of their mental and physical parts. He watched her breathe gently with a hint of a smile on her face and he wondered what she was dreaming. For a moment, he saw her as a father might have done...

No! He remonstrated with himself. *These thoughts should be and will be dismissed – think rather of the data pouring in, those brain sections all lining up – the last piece in the jigsaw... decades of work. What makes this girl the perfect subject,* he told himself, *is her flipping into the fifth dimension over a period of years. And she had nothing physically or mentally wrong with her – nothing to obscure the clarity of the results. How can you not do it?*

The professor turned to the orderlies in charge of the trolley.

"I want you to transport the subject to a secure location and have her regain consciousness. I need all drugs completely out of her system. She must be kept as calm as possible. Keep her happy; let her be with her friends because that will mitigate the stress levels. But watch them carefully – we cannot have them hurting themselves if they try to flip into the fifth dimension. That would be tragic."

Conscious? he thought. *A moment ago you were saying you could do this and succeed without that. Are you being fastidious – or maybe playing for time, delaying the inevitable?*

No. I'm not! He spoke sternly to himself. *This has to be done in precise clinical conditions.* He resolved there and then to put all weakness behind him. One might even think that he had been beginning to love the girl. Ridiculous!

29

Alice was the first to come to. She was alone in a place she did not recognise. She was clearly no longer at sea but in a small even-sided room. She lay on a bed, still wearing the designer dress she had been given on the boat.

The green world had completely vanished. It had to have been a dream but she could distinctly remember it - all of it. It was a land of pure truth - no deceiving of any kind was allowed. She had been forgiven all her guilty lies because she regretted them so much. Was she indeed forgiven? Was that the purpose of the dream? Where was she now?

The first thing she noticed from her prone position was a strip light in the middle of the ceiling but it was not turned on. The only light in the room came from a narrow window at ceiling level.

Alice did not like being alone. Once on dry land, they were going to try and flip. But to do that they needed to be together. She tapped the wall beside her, but it seemed pretty substantial. She rolled over and then felt sick. She got to her feet, staggered to the door and began pummelling it and screaming.

"Let me out. I need the bathroom. I feel sick."

Someone shouted something from the outside in a language she did not recognise and the door opened, revealing a man dressed entirely in black.

"Bath–" she began, but then couldn't hold it. She projected hot sick all over the man's chest."

"Ugh," he groaned.

If Alice had been able to see it – she was too mesmerised by the mess on the man's jacket – she would have seen a face filled with shock, horror and disgust. He screwed up his nose and uttered, *"Toalettet!"* and pulled her down a corridor, opened a door and pushed her inside without any ceremony or concern for someone so obviously unwell.

Charming, Alice thought. *But I suppose I did rather let him have it.* She took her time cleaning herself up. Fortunately, little of the mess had got onto her. She swilled her mouth – she didn't know whether the water was fit to drink.

Feeling better she looked around. Her thoughts had turned to escape – this man had not shown any sign of being her friend. There was a low cistern above the toilet. Above was another high window like the one in her room. But this window was open slightly; it was operated by a handle on the side. It may be possible to open it fully and for her to squeeze herself through. She knew, from the experience of getting through a window at home, that the problem was her head and hips but, if she could get her head through, and then make herself flat enough, all the rest of her would go, so long as the window was sufficiently wide. The one at home had not been and she got her hips stuck; it had taken both her mother and her father to get her back. But this window was as wide as the room. Escaping at that moment, though, would be the wrong time; she needed to know what was happening with the others.

She turned to the door to open it but it had been locked from the outside. She banged again and this time a woman in black approached with a stern, withering expression. She barked something at her and pulled at her arm. Alice tried to speak but the woman wasn't interested. She frog-marched her back up the corridor and thrust her back into her room.

"*Inn, jente!*"

Alice almost stepped in the vomit spatters on the floor. Another man, an older man, appeared and spoke quietly to the woman. "*Ingen skade, Hilda.*"

"Bah!" she expostulated.

Alice did not know what this language was, let alone understand it. It crossed her mind that she was on the flipside – these people reminded her of the Nazis she encountered in London. Where were her friends?

30

Hen stirred. He was aware of banging and a man yelling something beyond a door. He thought he recognised Norwegian. There had been a Norwegian girl at school for a couple of terms and he had picked up a few words. "*Ingen*" meant "none" and "*jente*" was "girl". One of the girls? He didn't understand the rest.

He was back on Earth. He had been sent back from witnessing the power of creation giving order and symmetry. It was not, he was sure, a figment of his imagination. One day, at the right time, he would return.

Where was he now? Not in the cabin - this room was on land. He had been drugged before the ship docked - presumably in the last meal they had been given. His head felt awful. He must think.

On land! They could be nearing the end, and, unless the prof had changed his mind, Nadia was first for the dissecting table. Where was she? The most important thing now was to find out where the others were.

Hen got up groggily and staggered to the door and banged on it. It opened almost immediately and a woman in black forced a bucket into his hands and then shut the door again.

It didn't take Hen long to realise what the bucket was for!

31

DI Renshaw straightened his back. It was a good feeling. In his hand was the picture of Prof W getting out of his car. "Yep. That's definitely him." He compared a still from the video taken by the NIS with one furnished by Mrs Brean. "So if our professor is entering that Norwegian warehouse, I'll bet my bottom dollar our young people are also there."

Up the line the message went until it reached the headquarters of the Norwegian Intelligence Service. Speed was necessary but with potential hostages, so was care.

A helicopter bearing crack troops trained in this kind of rescue was scrambled and within half an hour soldiers were advancing through the forest beside the road that led to the facility. Soon fifty men were deployed among trees just out of sight of the security cameras.

32

A woman in black with a huge bunch of keys unlocked Alice's door where she lay on her bed - there had not been a lot more for her to do - and barked, "*Opp, ute!*" The jailer gestured to the door.

Alice stood up and walked out of the door. She was shepherded to a kind of dining room where she was overjoyed to find Hen.

"Alice! You OK?" he asked, almost cuddling her but opting to take her upper arms instead.

"Yeah, fine... now. Was horribly sick back there. Must have been drugged but I got it all up... over the guard!" Alice uttered, with a hint of satisfaction.

"Yeah. I heard the swearing... you know it's Norwegian?"

"No," said Alice. "Are we in Norway, then?"

"Most likely. I can see pine trees out of the high window there. That would fit with being in Norway."

"Why Norway?"

"Why anywhere? Secure, maybe. I would surmise this is our final destination."

At that moment they were joined by Tom and Roxanne. They greeted each other with joyous shouts and Alice ran into Tom's open arms. The guards slammed the door and left them.

"Nadia! Where's Nadia?!" exclaimed Alice. Their joy was soon tempered by a huge sense of fear – they all knew it was Nadia that was to be the first. Alice shuddered. *Was Nadia already...?*

They stood in silence and waited. Ten minutes elapsed... fifteen... still no Nadia.

After twenty minutes, Alice mumbled, "Rox, she'll want you to say your prayers for her."

"Yeah," breathed Roxanne, quietly. "Now? Here?"

Alice nodded. "The sooner, the—"

But Alice was interrupted by a loud banging of a door at the end of the corridor and then Nadia's voice uttering or, rather, screaming all kinds of obscenities. The Norwegians were getting a rapid education in the kind of English that they would not have been taught in school. Most of it Alice didn't understand but it finished up with Nadia declaring, "Get your effing hands off of me you stinking pervert! If you think I'm going anywhere quietly with you, you've got another think coming... Go on, then. Shoot me! Let me have it... Better than the plans your boss has for me."

This was followed by more thumping and banging – the

security officer was clearly having difficulty with his charge.

"Nadia!" shouted Alice. "We're all here!"

Nadia desisted pummelling the man who was finding it hard obeying the order not to mark her.

The door opened and the battered-looking guard gave Nadia a final gentle push into the room. Nadia turned. "B*****" she called after him, as he gratefully pulled the door to.

"Brilliant! Great to see you lot." She was breathing heavily, her heart pounding and she collapsed into Roxanne's arms. "I thought they was... you know... and I weren't gonna go, like, quietly."

The female jailer of few words brought cans of coke and some sandwiches that smelled fishy. "*Spice...* Eat!" she ordered.

"Is this drugged?" demanded Hen, "like the last lot?"

The woman didn't seem to understand or want to be bothered to.

"Do you speak English?" asked Hen.

"Eat!" she commanded again and left.

"I think one of us should eat it first. Test it," suggested Tom. "I guess the Coke will be OK, though – the cans are sealed."

"Good idea," agreed Hen.

"I'll do it," volunteered Nadia.

"No Nadia," objected Hen. "It's you we most need to protect."

"Don't remind me! Should never have saved the effing prof."

"They'd have killed us, whatever," muttered Tom.

"Yes. Him being alive means we have to be preserved until he's ready," Hen reasoned. "And that's probably bought us some time... And, Nadia, would you have ever deliberately let a man die?"

"No. Would have felt bad forever... Anyway, I had this dream. It was, like, all rainbows and really beautiful... Don't laugh at me, guys, but, like, God was there. And He went, 'Nadia you're beautiful.' I told him not to be stupid but, you know what? He made me believe it. Said he never made, like, anything ugly. And, do you know what? I could'a stayed there forever - but my time ain't come, he said... Guess all the effing stuff they put into that food on the ship got to me brain. Hope it mucks it up for when the prof gets it."

"No, Nadia. I had a dream, too," said Roxanne. "It was, like, I was loved. There was this mother... Everywhere was, like, love forever... I don't think it was the drugs. I slipped through the grey slope in the fifth and it was this wonderful pink colour."

"For me it was blue - sky and sea," explained Tom. "It was pure goodness."

"Green," murmured Alice. "Green leaves and trees and grass for me - it was about truth. I was forgiven all my lies."

"And my world was yellow," smiled Hen. "It was an infinity of order and symmetry - a mathematical heaven but underlying it was a creative power that no science could ever test. We have, each of us, discovered something of the ultimate - the eternal that lies beneath the plane of the fifth... In fact, probably beneath everything - all that has been and all that will be - a timeless eternity... But we have all been sent back."

"Yeah," bounced Nadia, not feeling embarrassed any longer. "I were told I couldn't stay. I had a job to do."

"Great," declared Alice. "But guys, we do need to eat. Look, I was the first to wake up. I was sick and got it all up. Leave the sandwiches to me. After all, I'm supposed to be the one who goes in for the drugs."

Alice reached forward and took a sandwich and bit into it. "Not bad... Some kind of fish..." She took another bite, watching the others all waiting for her to keel over.

"Better wait... ten minutes," said Hen.

"Hey, Alice. What's all this about when you say 'the one going in for drugs'?" asked Roxanne. "You surprise me - never thought you would do drugs."

"I wouldn't, and I didn't," explained Alice, surprised by how much she still cared. What if she didn't make it back? "If I don't get home alive they'll think of me as being a cheat forever."

"How?..." Roxanne was confused.

"On the running track," put in Tom, "when she flipped... They asked her if she'd taken anything."

Alice became quite heated - the subject still clearly rankled her. "And I told them there was no way—"

"And there was no medical evidence whatsoever," continued Tom. "No one can say she was a drugs cheat. It would be a bare-faced lie."

"Some people don't listen to reason," shrugged Nadia. "It's the same with me."

"They're saying you were on drugs, too?" asked Roxanne.

"Nah. Not drugs. I flipped big time looking over the Avon Gorge... remember?"

Roxanne grimaced. "And, of course, they thought..."

"Yep. They all did... Apart from the doc in the hospital - he knew about the fifth. He gave me a fiver to get something to eat... oops, shouldn't have said that - he wanted me to keep it a secret."

"Shan't say anything," reassured Roxanne.

"Once someone thinks something about you, though, it will

always be there..." Alice said. Then she looked puzzled. "Look, Nadia, I don't get it. I'm not following this. We've been here before. What were they thinking? What has this place in Bristol got to do with anything?"

Nadia leaned forward and took her hand. "You don't get it because you're too good – in your mind. You think clean. That's why I didn't want to spell it out before."

"So, OK, I'm ready to be told, now. If Rox's in on it. Hen and Tom would probably like to know, too."

Tom looked at Hen. They nodded at each other. "I think we understand, Nadia," said Hen. "You were happy. You wouldn't have. We believe you."

"Thanks," said Nadia.

"You wouldn't have, what?" Alice almost shouted. "Everyone seems to know but me!"

Nadia sighed. "OK, Alice. What people do at the gorge is throw themselves over. It happens so often that there is even a notice up on the bridge with the Samaritans' number on it. People have been doing it, like, for... forever. It's a favourite place to end it all."

"What! You were thinking of committing suicide?!"

"NO," shouted Nadia, "I WASN'T! That's the frigging POINT. Everyone thinks I was, but I WASN'T. But it never occurred to you, Alice... and that's because it never crossed

155

your mind that anyone would want to do themselves in. You're good, Alice. You believed exactly what I said and weren't thinking I was telling a lie. That was great... and I wanted to keep it like that..."

Nadia continued quietly, "Topping yourself don't work. When someone launches themselves into the gorge, I always think of the poor sod who's got to scrape up the mess... If I did it - threw myself over - I wouldn't feel free; I'd be thinking of that poor sod. Once you think like that, you can't do it. Well, I couldn't. I ain't never going to kill myself no matter how bad it gets - or how beautiful I will be in God's land of rainbows. You see, for me, there has always been this other way out. Something like, good, somewhere. A kind of spark in the darkness. If you concentrate on that spark, you come out of it..."

No one said anything and Nadia went on. "My dad'd be a mess if I died - especially like that - he'd be screwed for sure. He tries to get *his* escape by doing drugs and drinking, but they don't work either; they only make it worse. What does work for him is having me to yell at... That's what he does - did - down the phone every night."

Nadia looked up at a silent Alice. Her mouth was open.

"I told you you weren't ready to hear it..."

Alice shook herself. "That's kind of scary. It makes me feel all cold just to think about it. But I'm glad you told me... So when the world gets, like, horrible and dark you see a light? A way out?"

"Yeah, a spark – that never goes out."

Alice got to her feet, "rainbows and sparks... Nadia, you *are* religious. That's, like, from the Bible somewhere."

"Is it? Nah, I ain't religious or nothing. But if there *is* a heaven with God in it, it has to be sparks and rainbows – a world with no poor people."

"Or wars... or research labs... biopsy needles... or Prof W," added Alice.

"Oh, he will be there," corrected Roxanne. "But only the *nice* side of him."

"Yeah," remembered Nadia. "The nice side that gives presents, like he did on my birthday... He didn't have to do that, did he?"

"No. I guess he likes you, really," said Hen.

"Well, he will in heaven. That's my idea, innit? Even if he chops my brain to bits."

Alice shuddered again. She didn't want to think of that. Then she remembered that she had finished eating and none of the others had begun. "Oh, sorry. I quite forgot – I'm still awake it seems and I have no stomach ache or anything so I don't think this is poisoned."

"Let's eat. I'm hungry," declared Tom. "And after we've finished, now we are together, we could try and flip."

"Agreed," affirmed Hen.

33

Their stomachs full, the five friends joined hands and tried to bring on a flip. Only Roxanne and Alice could summon up anything but they couldn't sustain it and they re-entered the room with a heavy thump.

"Ow!" grumbled Alice. "I'm sorry guys. This is not going to work, is it?"

"We're not in the best of health," explained Hen. "Not enough energy."

"Guess so," agreed Tom. "I didn't get anywhere. The harder I try, the less likely it is to happen. So what are we going to do? I feel more trapped than ever, now."

They sat in silence for several minutes, then Alice spoke. "You know the bathroom. Have you seen the window?"

"Yes," nodded Hen, "too high and narrow to get out of."

"For you, maybe. But I think I could do it."

"I definitely couldn't," said Tom. "We stick together, remember. If we split up..." He did not want to let Alice out of his sight.

Alice sighed. "I agree. But perhaps the time has come for

one of us to get out to summon help. It's now or never – desperate measures time, isn't it?"

When not even Nadia put in an objection, Alice continued. "In this world, the authorities are supposed to be on our side, aren't they? Somehow, if I was on my own – in Norway – I bet the people I met would send for the police."

"Running through the streets dressed like that, they'd have you down for a prostitute," mumbled Tom.

"Thanks!" Alice folded her arms, crossly.

Hen, who was far more used to skimpy fashions rarely encountered in West Bay, sprang to her rescue. "Or someone from a high society cocktail party. I think... I think... I think that you may be right, Alice... Look, we're getting near the end. They're not going to just keep us and feed us forever. Alice is right; it's time for desperate measures."

"I could go as soon as it gets dark and..." Alice suddenly felt the import of what she was proposing. For the first time since she had left home, she was planning to venture out and do something on her own – and it was dangerous. The others knew it, too. And she was right and Hen, the wise one, agreed with her. Time was running out. It was now or never. Would she be brave enough? She had a moment of regret and deep inside herself began to panic. *Maybe I shouldn't have volunteered... but it's too late now*, she told herself.

160

Flip! The Daisychain

"When it's dark, then," confirmed Hen.

The jailer turned up with a box of board games.

"For - you - to - play," she said in stilted English, with a scowl.

"Thanks. *Takk*," said Hen.

The woman looked at him, "*Kan du norsk?*"

"*Nei*. I knew a Norwegian girl once, that's all."

The woman shrugged and left.

"That confirms it. We're definitely somewhere in Norway," pronounced Hen.

"Is there no limit to your powers?" joked Alice, brightly, but inside she was nervous... dead nervous... no, scared!

Hen replied. "Yes, Alice. I have severe limitations. In this case, I'm too big to get through the loo window. Look after yourself; we need you."

"Don't worry, I will," Alice assured him, as confidently as she could.

Half an hour later they saw the light from the high window begin to fade.

"When I win this game of Ludo, I'm going," announced Alice bravely.

After ten minutes, and having come last in the game, Alice

161

straightened up. "Saving all my luck for the next game." She spoke lightly. "Right. Tom, you're to say you're feeling sick. They don't like that. Then, when they're attending to you, I will yell for the bathroom. With a bit of luck, she'll not miss me until I'm right away from the building."

"And when she does, we'll keep her quiet," promised Roxanne.

Tom began to call. The others made noises and the woman in black strode in, keys jangling.

"*Du, stille!*"

"I feel sick," spluttered Tom, and in an act that would have won him an Oscar, he fell on his knees.

"*Nei!*" yelled the woman. She stepped forward. At the same time, Alice clutched her stomach and grunted. "I need the bathroom!"

The jailer stood, assessed the situation, rushed to the toilet and unlocked the door, then returned to Tom. The plan was working. Alice closed the door and locked it from the inside. Then she operated the lever, opening the window to its fullest extent.

Stepping onto the toilet seat, she climbed onto the cistern lid and reached up. She was a couple of centimetres too short. Almost off balance, she managed to grasp the rods that operated the opening mechanism with her right hand and yanked herself up just enough to catch the sill with her left. Straining with every muscle, she swung her right arm up, too, and, then, with all her might, she got her left hand through the window and grasped the outside of the windowsill. She was now fully committed; there was no going back – her feet were well clear of the cistern lid and if she let go, she would fall all the way to the floor. A wave of fear passed through her.

Desperately, Alice called up some superhuman strength from somewhere and managed to get her right arm through, too. Now her face was at window level. She lowered her head to the left and put it through the hole. To fall back now would prove very nasty, even fatal – she would almost certainly break her neck. "Do not try this at home!" she grunted under her breath and tried to overcome her fear. She could now look down the outside wall and was delighted to find a pipe within grasping distance; she reached for it and, with both hands on it, pulled her chest through. The low neck of the dress caught on the sill and tore, but all her upper half was now through; her waist bent across the ledge. She was head down but the ground on the outside was higher than the inside floor. With a mighty tug, she got her hips up to the windowsill. Her bottom stuck on the top of the inside of the open window but, with one last wrench on the pipe, Alice slid through.

Fortunately, the ground was covered in myrtle and the thick bushes broke her fall. She was battered, bruised, bleeding from a scrape on her leg and covered in multiple scratches inflicted by the bushes. She had left one shoe and most of her dress behind. But she was through - outside. Free!

Alice struggled to her feet - the bushes impeded her but nothing appeared to be broken. She was out, alive. She stood and gathered her breath, deciding which way to run.

Then Alice heard the sounds of commotion from inside the toilet. Her escape had been noticed! But she could hear Hen and Tom's raised voices. She had to make good her escape. The jailer swore but her words were curtailed and Alice saw Hen's hand at the window. He must have clambered onto the cistern. "You OK, Alice?" he called.

"Yeah. I'm on my way," she replied softly, as she turned to run up the myrtle-covered slope towards a line of pines.

She hadn't gone far, however, before she saw three men in black uniform come around an illuminated corner of the warehouse behind her. They began to scramble through the bushes toward the place she had escaped from. *Oh no, I must have been caught on CCTV or something.* If only she were dressed in black, too - virtually naked, her pale skin must have shone clearly in the same moonlight that was helping her see what was in front of her. She ducked down behind some myrtle bushes just as a powerful torchlight split the darkness to her left. The beam swung across but returned to the left of her - she hadn't been seen.

As the black-clad figures advanced to her left, Alice scrambled up the slope towards a line of trees on the right – if only she could make the trees she may still get away. Then, at last, the torch beam engulfed her and the black figures shouted at her to stop. She ignored them and clambered on with even greater speed. The beam persisted. It helped her find her way and she scampered desperately, powered by the adrenalin of fear. To her relief, the men didn't seem to be gaining on her. Maybe, just maybe...

Am I dreaming? she thought. *Is this really happening?* If it was a nightmare, then it was the most vivid one she had ever had. She made the trees... then, out of nowhere, a gloved hand shot out and closed over her mouth and a second around her waist lifted her off her feet and pulled her out of the glare of the torchlight into a shallow hollow.

Dressed in camouflage fatigues, the soldier had been completely invisible. He turned her to face him but kept his hand over her mouth. He seemed huge and immensely strong and she stared at him in terror. But then he gently released his grip on her waist and put his forefinger to his lips and whispered, "You, safe. Quiet." For some reason, Alice's mind was filled with memories of *Shrek*. In the moonlight, the man looked that big. "You stay quiet?" Alice nodded and the soldier took his hand from her mouth. He pushed her down lower behind the bushes and she became aware of other soldiers there, too. They stepped over her and positioned themselves between her and her pursuers who were noisily searching for Alice – one of them calling on her to give herself up.

Then, suddenly, the calling stopped and she heard a thud as a heavy torch hit a fallen branch and tumbled onto the ground. She had a fleeting glimpse of a soldier before the light went out. More brief thumps followed and all was still.

Alice wanted to do something, say something, but the very silence seemed to bind her lips. After a few minutes, which felt like a very long time, she heard the sounds of the night in the forest start up and come back to life.

The soldiers took Alice further up the slope through the trees to where a commander crouched. "How many others? Inside how many of you teenagers?"

"Four," said Alice, trembling. "Four others." Should she have lied? But had it not been her that had said people in this world would be on their side?

"All alive?"

"Yes," answered Alice. "Who are you?"

"Norway Army. You are safe. We rescue you. Where are your friends?"

"That side of the building, there." She pointed. "Where I

escaped from."

"They are together?"

"Yes, all in one room. At least they were when I escaped but now they know I've gone, they might move them."

"OK. You are safe." He took off his outer jacket and put it over her bare shoulders.

34

In Arlington, the FBI, now armed with the certain knowledge that Padget was fully implicated in the Daisychain movement, had removed his wife and family for questioning and the house was being taken apart. But so far they had found nothing to suggest his involvement in anything other than his legitimate businesses, and his wife, it appeared, had no idea he was no longer in Scotland. Where was he?

MI5 had turned up a vital clue. Padget's driver had taken him to Glasgow Central Station but none of the CCTV pictures showed him inside the concourse or on the platforms. But a few days before, he had arrived at Prestwick. What if he had decided to use the airport again?

Yes, there was footage of him hailing a taxi and then again in the airport terminal. After a detailed study of passenger lists, they had uncovered his flight to Paris and the French internal security, DGSI, were now also on the case. The international community had fully woken up to the potential impact of the Daisychain.

35

Unaware of what was happening outside, Prof W undressed and got into his bed. It wasn't a bad bed, but sleep didn't come easily. He was dog-tired but in the dark, he couldn't get the picture of Nadia lying on the trolley waiting for him out of his mind. Eventually, exhausted, he nodded off.

The next thing he was aware of was that he was sitting upright clearing his head of a nightmare. In it, the prone Nadia had opened her eyes and looked at him the way she had done when she had tended him as *he* lay on *his* back on the soil of the island.

No, he told himself, *it's no good I can't do it. Tomorrow, when I have prepared the syringe it won't be for her; it will be for me. Maybe God - if there is a God - will have mercy on me. The Lord knows I began all this with the purest of intentions.*

He lay down and closed his eyes and the face of the girl wore a smile. *If I had had children - been less obsessed with science and more on family life... if I had had children they would be the age of these teenagers. I guess this is the nearest I have been to being a parent.*

As their professor was contemplating his own death, Tom had their jailer face down on the bathroom floor with a towel across her mouth trying to stifle her screams. Hen had pulled off his shirt and Nadia was using it to tie the woman's hands as Hen grasped her wrists behind her back.

"Your shirt, too, Tom," ordered Nadia. She pulled his shirt up and he put each arm up in turn as Nadia took it over his head. Hen paid attention to the woman's ankles and Nadia obliged with the same kind of knot that seemed to work on the hands.

Tom fixed the towel to keep the woman's noise down but not so as to prevent her from breathing. Together they lifted her into the bathtub where she continued to squirm and pound with her feet. The three shut the bathroom door and returned to the room with the table. The Ludo set seemed an odd thing as they thought and prayed for Alice.

"She may be back in a few minutes," mumbled Nadia.

"No. She's resourceful," said Tom. He was determined to be positive.

"Didn't say she wasn't," retorted Nadia.

"Let's not meet the bad news before we have to," advised Hen, quietly. "Let's see if we can find somewhere to hide."

They tried the jailer's keys in the door that led into the rest of the facility. Eventually, they found the right one. But as the key turned, several black-clad figures burst in and thrust the young people back into the room.

36

The senior officer of the Norwegian commandos remarked to his junior, "For a warehouse, this place has an unbelievable number of security cameras. Every corner is monitored. There will be a rear exit for certain so I want the land and woods behind the facility monitored as we begin the frontal assault." An order was passed to the troops hidden in the woods to the rear: "Hold your positions, be alert for a possible back door."

Inside, unaware of the soldiers' presence, the security room staff were becoming anxious at the failure of the men who had gone out in pursuit of Alice to report in. Their eyes were fixed on the screens as they scanned the woods and then consternation grew to alarm when the commander of the commandos gave the order and snipers began taking out the "eyes" of the enemy.

The security room staff watched as one by one their screens blanked out. Within thirty seconds, all the forward-looking cameras had been disabled by gunfire from the trees. They had no idea of the size of the assault force, nor who the perpetrators were – they had received no intelligence that their facility was about to be attacked; those going about their business in the way they had done for months were caught completely off-guard.

"Probably pranksters," declared the chief. "Return fire into the woods. Let 'em have it."

The soldiers were quite aware that a blind enemy would strike out – a wounded beast is a dangerous one. But his men were ready for this and replied with a volley of tear gas into the open front loading bay . The roll-doors to the warehouse began to descend but stopped short of the ground as the CS gas rose and the shooting from within ceased.

Aware, now, that this was no band of pranksters and it would only be a matter of time before they were overrun, the leadership issued the order for the immediate evacuation of the élite. Their monitors showed no assailants to the rear. The back door was a tunnel that led up into the trees, exiting through a bank of bushes and undergrowth that was not immediately visible. In the dark, it would see the Daisychain leadership well on their way to boats nestled in the harbour on the other side of the small headland.

But they did not plan against an army equipped with night vision. As they began to emerge from the tunnel entrance, the infrared radiation from their warm bodies was instantly detected by the soldiers' night vision equipment. Within five minutes the first group was surrounded. Seeing soldiers armed to the teeth, those attempting to escape quickly surrendered.

Now the soldiers had a way into the heart of the facility from the rear. At the front, the first soldiers were already entering through the smoke.

Almost at the same time as they had been thrust back into the their room, Nadia, Hen, Roxanne and Tom heard the gunfire begin. The men in black left immediately, leaving the jailer still trussed up in the bath. But the four friends could go nowhere – the door to their room was firmly locked. As explosions rocked the building, all they could do amid the noise and the din was to lie flat on the floor under the table. The jailer gave up kicking and grunting, and lay still, terrified.

"Is this all down to Alice?" asked Nadia.

Hen didn't think so. "Can't be. Whatever this is about, it's all happened too fast for it to be anything to do with Alice, I reckon."

"Hope she's all right," muttered Roxanne. "I mean outside, with all this going on, may not be the safest place."

"She's sensible," murmured Tom. "She'll keep her head down that's for sure." Inside, his heart was screaming but he was determined not to show it. He tried to tell himself that Alice had actually escaped to safety from the guns that seemed to be all around them. "I reckon they were already watching this place and Alice got 'em going."

"Maybe," said Hen.

37

In the moments before the assault, Prof W had lain awake; his tired brain reflecting on his decision to opt out of life. Suicide becomes increasingly inviting as a person becomes more exhausted or trapped, and Reginald Williams was both. He was exercised as to what might become of the young people when he was no longer around. Was there some way he could help them escape? He couldn't think of any.

Then, without warning and completely unexpectedly, a cacophony of gunfire broke into his consciousness. He sat up once more. No, he hadn't dreamed it. Silence had resumed for a few seconds but then the guns began again – this time in earnest. It was like an answer to an unspoken prayer.

He quickly made himself decent and stepped out of his room. Hardly knowing which way to turn, he made his way to the control room. When he arrived it was full of the smell of tear gas. As he entered, the main doors opposite opened and black-clad defenders rushed through.

A deafening blast shook the table and a set of files slid to the floor. Then a second explosion shattered the doorway and the professor ducked down among the paper and books - a computer keyboard hung from its lead and swung in the space between desk and floor, colliding gently with his head.

Armed men fell back into the control room and fled passed him up the corridor from which he had entered. He had no idea where they were going and where they expected to take up positions. He just crouched there, shocked and bemused. Then he spotted a soldier in combat camouflage gear dash through the shattered doorway. A volley of fire from behind fizzed passed the professor's head and right shoulder, narrowly missing him but strafing the advancing soldier, hitting him in the thigh and elbow. The soldier spun around and hit the floor right in front of Prof W.

Instinctively, the doctor in him sprang into life. He had already written off his own life; safety was not his primary concern. He had nowhere to run in any case.

Blood was spurting out of a wound high on the soldier's leg. It had to be stopped. He knelt beside the man and lifted the leg onto his own. Direct pressure was needed but the bullet had passed right through. Williams pushed up into the groin and found the main femoral artery and applied as much force as he could. The gushing slowed. A tourniquet? Taking the soldier's uninjured hand, he pushed it into the place where his own fingers were. "Press here... hard!" The soldier obeyed. "Er du lege? Doctor?" he uttered.

"Neurologist... Don't let go!" ordered the professor.

The soldier had no idea what he was talking about but he kept pressing – he knew this civilian was trying to save his life. Prof W pulled off the soldier's boot and calf-length sock and began to tie the latter tightly above the wound in his thigh. The blood ceased to flow. Prof W now checked the man's left hand and lower arm. The bones were shattered but the arteries appeared to be holding. He straightened the limb carefully, then reached up and pulled a soft plastic-covered file from the floor behind him, wrapped it around the arm and tied it gently with the soldier's other sock.

Prof W was vaguely aware of camouflage racing past him in pursuit of the fleeing defenders. Then a fresh cloud of tear gas seeped over him. The soldier grunted and motioned to his side with his head. "*Maske,*" he uttered. Prof W saw immediately what he was on about – a mask to protect him from the tear gas. He pulled it out and made to put it on the soldier. The soldier shook his head. "*Nei, du ... Du legen.*" Then the soldier relaxed. His ability to remain conscious was seeping from him.

Williams obeyed. If he was to help this man and maybe others he did not need to be disabled by tear gas. A boot came into his vision beside the casualty – a soldier bent down and felt his comrade's pulse.

"This man needs hospital or he will die... now!" declared Prof W, lifting his mask. The officer shouted an order and two men arrived with a stretcher, lifted the wounded soldier and carried him out towards the front of the building. The professor followed.

Outside Prof W removed the mask and began checking two other wounded men. A sudden surge of the realisation of the futility of it all struck him. Three healthy young men with serious wounds - and goodness knows how many others inside the building. He thought of the young people - his charges - teenagers who had been entrusted to him by their parents. Once again, as he held a man with a bullet wound to his abdomen, he was back on the island, Nadia bending over him, giving him care, saving his life. Tears welled up - and not at that moment just because of the gas.

"Five young people... inside," he said to one of the soldiers tending the wounded with him. "They must not be hurt." The soldier passed the message on in Norwegian. A commander looked across and approached.

"What can you tell me of young people?"

"Five teenagers. They were kidnapped and brought here... from London."

"Where are they?"

"Inside. I don't know where."

"And you are?"

"Reginald Williams. Their neur— their doctor. I was taken, too." *Which is not entirely untrue,* he reflected. "Trapped," he added.

The shooting got nearer and the four friends huddled together under their table. Then they smelled tear-gas seeping under the door and decided the floor was not the best place. Whatever it was that was going on outside they hoped Alice was not caught up in it.

Suddenly, there was a burst of gunfire within metres of the room in which they were imprisoned. Men's voices, speaking Norwegian, sounded outside. Crack... crash! The door from the outside burst open and heavy booted soldiers ran into the section, kicking open the doors of the rooms in turn. Nadia, Hen, Roxanne and Tom stood against the wall – their hands in the air in the semi-darkness. Could this be the way they die?

"*På gulvet!*" barked a uniform. "Floor!"? The four were forced to lay face-down on the floor. Roxanne began spluttering.

"We're not armed," pleaded Hen.

Then there was a sound of laughter. One of the soldiers had entered the bathroom and seen the jailer tied and gagged lying in the bathtub. Her face was the picture of terror. The soldier spoke with levity in Norwegian; an expression that the friends later learned was something along the lines of: "Don't worry lady. It seems you've already been dealt with."

38

From beginning to end, the battle barely lasted fifteen minutes but, for those caught up in it, it seemed much longer than that. After the guns ceased, helicopters landed and the casualties were airlifted to the hospital in Ålesund. It was remarkable how few casualties among the soldiers there were. The defenders were not so lucky. The professor was deployed to tend to them. Three were dead. Others were critical; several would lose limbs if they survived. The neurologist watched them go in a succession of ambulances and a helicopter.

At last, the four young people were brought out of the building and led to an ambulance in the car park in front of the building. Alice was waiting for them. She screamed her delight as she leapt to embrace Tom. They hugged and wept and jumped with joy. They were all reunited and all alive... free! There was nothing any of them could do to hold back as, in each other's arms, they hurtled into their world of new dimensions.

Prof W saw them collapse in a heap. He rushed over to where the paramedics, taken completely by surprise, were trying to separate the bodies and feel for pulses. One of them jumped down from the ambulance with a defibrillator.

"No. You'll not need that," shouted the professor. "?They are all right. It will pass. We must keep them still." Seeing them there, his mind lurched to thinking of the state-of-the-art scanner not a hundred metres away inside the facility. Never had he had an opportunity like this. It was remarkable that they all flipped together at the same time – this was something he hadn't anticipated. What had he missed? Could it be that it was centred in the shell of the nucleus accumbens rather than the parietal lobe as he had previously decided, based on all the insufficient evidence he had had to hand? He would need to scan immediately and see where their brains lit up; his own dopamine began to flow as his scientific curiosity was seriously stimulated.

But before the professor could begin to explain, to the soldiers' amazement, the five young people just melted away and the professor wondered if he would ever see them again.

Within the fifth, the five friends linked arms. Normal speech was impossible – as was four-dimensional hearing – but they had learned to communicate fluently through the kind of telepathy they had discovered. Hen was saying/thinking.

"Better keep abreast of the spheres, we do not want to travel back or forward in time."

Alice couldn't help letting on how anxious she was to see her family.

And Tom sent, "Guys, Let's not stay too long."

Then Hen sent in his wise tone. "We need to go back and help them sort out everything. Then, afterwards, we can all flip in peace as much as we like and research things properly."

"Yeah," communicated Roxanne. "I'm a free person! Nobody's ever going to take that away from me."

That made Tom think. "We'll have to get back to exactly where we left," he intimated.

Hen agreed. "Time to go back. We don't want to get lost."

Holding each other tightly, they slid through the vortex and, splayed on the ground, they re-entered the four dimensions of the dusty Norwegian car park.

Professor Williams reached out and took Nadia's limp hand in his – not as a doctor assessing her condition, but now like a father full of concern. He let go of her hand as she came to.

Hen sat up. "Sorry about that. Just too much excitement. I guess, we all decided not to resist it this time."

Prof W was amazed. "So you can control this? When you flip. How long you go for, and where you re-emerge?"

"Professor," said Hen, calmly. "There is so much you don't understand about the fifth. We've been telling you for months but you just wouldn't listen. Flipping is a gift, not a disease. And it is more than a neurological phenomenon controlled by a few peptides. It stands to reason that anything that can take us into a parallel universe has to have its origins outside human interior experience."

"Parallel universe?" The professor's face said it all.

"Yes," said Hen. "The fifth has much more than you ever began to suspect – even in your wildest dreams. Donald Padget has more awareness of the power of this than you."

The professor was thrown and said nothing in reply as he tried to regain his scientific sea-legs in the field of neurology in which he had sought his reputation. He felt he had to say something but, at that moment, he realised that he knew far less than he had ever realised and did not know what to say. He looked at the soldiers staring at him, searching for an explanation of what this was all about. All he managed was, "I think you will find that they are quite all right now. This phenomenon is not one that appears to leave the subjects in any kind of distress or confusion. It is what I... and they... have been studying, and what this corrupt organisation that you see here wanted to possess."

Alice got to her feet, knocking grit off her scantily dressed backside, and stared Prof W in the eye. "Whose side are you on, professor?" she demanded, curtly.

"Yours. I wouldn't want you hurt," he mumbled.

"Changed your tune, ain't you?" shot Nadia, crossly.

"I never wanted you to come to any harm... I just wanted to—"

"Finish your paper and get your recognition," Hen finished for him.

"Yes. But I couldn't do that. Not since I learned... since you saved my life on that island. You could have let me die to save yourselves, but you didn't. You came back and rescued me and Wood."

"Course," dismissed Nadia.

Prof W looked down at his feet. "Out of the mouths of babes and infants..." he murmured.

"Eh?" Nadia wasn't sure what he meant. "What you on about?"

"Nothing."

"If you're talking about *us*, we ain't babies!"

"No," declared the professor. "Far from it." *But, nevertheless,* he thought, *you have a childlike innocence that I hope you will never lose.*

"Doctor," interrupted a paramedic. "We need to take these people to the hospital. They have superficial wounds that need attending to." He looked especially at a blood-smeared Alice who was still clasping the army officer's jacket across her shoulders.

Suddenly, there was a clatter of boots across the threshold of the facility. Soldiers were running from the building as fast as their legs would carry them.

"*Legg der ned!* Booby-trapped!" shouted the lead soldier. Everyone hit the deck. Once again Alice felt the grit of the car park dig into her bare legs.

Then, "Boom! Boom! Boom!" The facility was rocked by a series of explosions; flames and debris flew out of the main doors and the roof lifted. Within minutes the whole building was a blazing inferno. The Daisychain had no intention of allowing its secrets to be revealed.

39

When they heard that all five had passed out in the car park, the doctors in the hospital in Ålesund wanted to keep them overnight for observation. The friends asked to be discharged but the hospital doctor would not allow them to leave without their parents or guardians. Their people would have to come to them.

☆☆☆

In the Winterford, the phone rang. It was Scotland Yard. The young people and the professor had been found in Norway – in Ålesund. They were all alive and well. At first, their families were stunned – the news caught them by surprise – but, as it sank in, they exploded with joy.

DI Renshaw headed immediately to the Winterford.

"If any of the relatives want to go to Norway, I can arrange that," he explained. "Scotland Yard will send a car to transport you to Gatwick where you can join a direct flight to Ålesund. On arrival at Vigra airport, you will be met by the

British consul and taken to a hotel.

"What about Professor Williams, Inspector?" demanded Mrs Brean, against the hubbub of relief and celebration of the families as they hugged each other, wept and rejoiced.

"He is in one piece. It appears he is being taken to Oslo for questioning."

"Why? He is a victim of all this, too."

"If he is, then I am sure he has nothing to worry about, Mrs Brean. You *have* told us all you know haven't you?"

"Yes. Well. He was in financial difficulties and a man called Donald Padget lent him money. Perhaps I should have told you that?"

"Yes, Mrs Brean, you should have. It took us a little research to discover his relationship to Donald Padget – time that could well have seen the deaths of innocent young people and even, perhaps, your dear professor himself."

"It didn't seem... that important..."

"His debts took away his freedom, Mrs Brean, and anything that does that renders a person vulnerable."

"I'm sorry, Inspector."

"Save your apologies for the judge."

"Am I to be charged?"

"Not yet."

"Thank you."

"Don't thank me, Mrs Brean. Thank your lucky stars that these youngsters have been found fit and well."

"I do, Inspector. Indeed, I do."

Bishop Rowena, joining the conversation, said, quietly, "I don't believe in lucky stars, Inspector, but I do have One I can thank. May I book a seat on the plane to Ålesund, too? I hope that is all right."

"Perfectly, if your people in the United States can spare you. If you hadn't picked up on this so quickly, Bishop, five young persons and their professor would probably be dead by now. And from what I hear, they have led the authorities to uncover a threat to international security that is way beyond anything we had ever imagined."

"Oh. Do call me Rowena... One thing led to another?"

"Suffice it to say that it involves MI5, MI6, your FBI and CIA, I believe, and the intelligence agencies of at least two other countries, almost certainly more. People are being arrested around the world as we speak."

☆☆☆

Unaware of what had happened in Ålesund, a big white yacht pulled into Reykjavik harbour, Iceland - the port in which it was registered. Before the crew could disembark, however, the Icelandic police boarded and impounded the vessel. The entire crew were arrested and remanded in custody and the vessel searched. To everyone's amazement, locked in an inside cabin was a man in Scottish fisherman's gear. He was in a bad way, but alive.

As the families of Alice, Tom, Nadia and Hen were landing in Norway, a confused but delighted wife of an Ullapool fisherman was flying out to Iceland to be reunited with her husband. She had thought of him on the seabed somewhere within sight of the Scottish coast. Now, after many days, he had turned up alive in Reykjavik.

There had been a distrust of Icelandic fishermen ever since the Cod Wars ended in the 1970s, but never before had anyone made quite such an unexpected journey into enemy territory. A local reporter, keen to make a name for himself, weighed into the mystery, only to be told that the information he was after was classified. "Lost Ullapool fisherman rescued by luxury yacht and taken to Iceland," began his article but he could tell his readers little else.

40

Alice's parents, Tom's mum, Nadia's dad and even Hen's parents from Abu Dhabi rushed into the lobby of the hospital to greet their children. There was no one, however, to greet Roxanne, who stood aside and watched the mêlée. The British consul approached and introduced himself to her.

"Your people are not here?"

"I don't have any. Before I went to the Winterford clinic, I was with some foster parents but only for a few months. Don't worry, I'm used to it."

Before the consul could say anything, however, Nadia had rushed across to introduce Rox to her father. Hen had turned his attention to the others, too, and Alice had dragged her parents towards Tom and his mum.

"Rox is going to live with us!" announced Nadia. "She ain't got no one but us."

"But Nadia, it ain't as easy—" began Roxanne.

"All for one and one for all!" declared her friend. "That means, like, forever!"

Rowena stood smiling in the doorway.

"Ro!" yelled Nadia. And she, Hen, Alice and Tom surrounded her.

"You got my message?!" exclaimed Hen.

"You don't like cheesy-chips," Rowena laughed. "And this, I gather, will be Roxanne. I've heard a lot about you. I'm pleased to meet you."

The British consul negotiated the necessary paperwork and, at last, the five were released into the care of their elders. Taking Nadia's lead, the consul had linked Roxanne with her. They left the hospital and moved on to a pleasant hotel nearby.

Over the next hour in the hotel lounge, the five learned what had transpired following Hen's distress call and their disappearance. The bishop explained that they had to thank Mel at the youth club and her boss, the vicar.

"She only met us once," explained Hen.

"We should go back and thank them," suggested Alice.

"Well, you clearly made an impression," smiled Rowena.

"Shouldn't you be in America?" asked Alice.

"What and miss all the excitement! I'm on holiday... extended holiday. And now I want to hear your story from beginning to end. We know that you turned up in Scotland but how did you get there? Where did you meet up with Roxanne?"

"How long have you got?" laughed Hen. "There is a lot more to the fifth than anyone can guess... too much to go into here. But, suffice it to say, that turning up in Inverlochie was a pure accident."

Alice's dad was growing impatient. "There's a plane that leaves for Amsterdam in two hours. From there we can connect direct to Leeds-Bradford airport. We can be home within five hours. We are grateful to you," he said to the consul, "but we would rather get home than stay here and return to Gatwick which is a long way from our home in Leeds."

Alice couldn't ever put into words exactly what she felt at that moment. She had been fighting homesickness for much of their time but now the thought of leaving her four friends so abruptly - especially Tom - was appalling.

To her parents' complete surprise and horror, Alice's expressive face showed a degree of defiance they had never witnessed before. They had known their Alice to be resilient and determined - she had shown it in her athletics training - but they had never known her to be wilful. Alice simply said, "No!" loudly and with a tone of complete finality.

Her dad was caught by surprise and it took him a few moments to recover. He was trying to find the words to override her objection but his wife laid her hand on his arm and said, calmly, "I think Alice has to go through, what do they

call it, a debrief or something when she gets back, darling."
She looked questioningly at the consul.

"I do not know for certain what will happen in Britain," he
answered, "but my orders are to see that you are rested and
then, if fit, I am to arrange for you to all fly back to Gatwick.
Any other arrangement will have to be cleared by my
superiors."

Alice breathed a huge sigh of relief that was not inaudible.
Tom looked across at her and their eyes met. There was no
way that either of them would ever be content with their old
homes again. When it came to it, Alice thought, her parents
would perhaps be more understanding than Tom's mum, who
had envisaged her son with her in her small seaside village for
the rest of her life.

Looking back, that was the moment when Alice recognised
that she and Tom were bound to each other, come what may.
They had shared so much that no one else outside the group
could ever truly understand and she realised that she couldn't
simply go back to her old life.

Bishop Rowena understood all this. She decided to
intervene. "It is a tremendous relief to us all that these young
people are reunited with those who love them. But, I fear, the
game is not yet over. If I have read the situation correctly," she
looked up at Hen, "what has happened here is but the tip of

the iceberg. I gather you have encountered an unsavoury American called Donald Padget."

"Yeah," broke in Nadia, "he was in the Winterford and we saw him in that castle in Scotland."

"Inverlochie," supplied Hen. "He's part of the international Daisychain."

"But," said Rowena, "I understand he was not there when the police arrived. So, he's on the loose somewhere. And until he's apprehended, I would say that you all should remain on your guard... Mr and Mrs Downey, I wouldn't recommend taking your daughter home just get."

Later that night, as she lay in the bed in the hotel, Alice got to thinking, *I've, kind of, like, fledged; haven't I? Somehow, I'm not desperate to go home anymore.*

41

The following day they arrived at Vigra airport to take the plane to Gatwick. In the departure lounge, Hen called a meeting of the five friends. Again, Bishop Rowena mollified the protective parents who didn't like being excluded. She explained that their young people had to go through the process of coming to terms with what had happened together and alone.

"My parents don't like being left out," reported Alice.

Hen came to their defence. "You can't blame them, Alice. They've gone through a lot not knowing where you were. They don't want to lose you again."

"Bishop Rowena's good, though," affirmed Tom. "You can see my mum trusts her."

Roxanne spoke up. "Look, guys. You know I haven't got any of these ties. Make the most of them. All I've got to look forward to is the vain hope the council will give me a flat somewhere, or else I will be put in another foster home."

"Nah! That ain't gonna happen, Rox!" thundered Nadia. "You're coming to stay with me, ain't ya. Unless you—"

"But Nadia, I can't just move in like—"

"Yeah, you can," Alice declared. She surprised even herself. "Look, Rox. Nadia needs you. What with her dad and all. She needs a sister."

Nadia applauded Alice's support. "Well put, Alice. That's settled, then. You're my sister, innit?"

"Well... OK. If you really mean—"

"Course I do!" interjected Nadia as firmly as she could.

"Nadia means it, Rox," insisted Alice.

"I would say that the ayes have it," pronounced Hen, as if he were announcing the results of a vote from the Speaker's chair. "Rox is now officially Nadia's adopted sister."

Tom became solemn. "After the past few months, we're *all* like brothers and sisters of the 5D; No one's been on the journey we have. In fact, how many of us have told our people about the flipside – I mean the Nazis being in charge in our parallel world?"

They all knew the answer: None of them. The reasons mainly centred on the difficulty of where to begin. They would be thought of as just bonkers for sure. And there were all sorts of other reasons that made it hard to talk about.

"And I don't want to frighten my parents any more than they have been already," whispered Alice, glancing over her shoulder at the group of parents and officials. "If they believed me, they would try to ground me for life."

Roxanne had no one to tell and no desire to tell anyone.

Nadia said her father had a problem with thinking about anything outside of the few streets in which he lived. If he had found himself south of Bristol's Floating Harbour, she reckoned he would think he was already in a parallel world.

The defeat of the Nazis for Tom's mother was a vindication of what her parents had been through. "It would break her heart to think that the Germans had landed in West Bay," he concluded.

Hen tried to be logical. "But we can't keep it a secret forever, can we? Reluctant as we are, I think we will have to share it. It's how we do it and with whom that matters. I think we should do it officially with someone first - someone who might understand."

Alice knew Hen was right. She couldn't just deny a very significant part of her young life and never ever talk about it. It was OK while she was with the others but after that it would just drive her mad to pretend all those things never happened. "Yeah, but who?" she asked. "There are not many people who have a clue about the *first* thing of what the fifth is about, let alone a flipside. Not even Prof W."

"But there is someone," suggested Hen. "Bishop Ro is here and doing what she is because she believes in it. She got to know about it through my parents but it was when she went to see that professor in New York who is researching 5D that she got convinced. He might be a good person to begin telling."

"So you reckon if we collared him and told him about the Nazis, he would understand?" asked Nadia.

Hen nodded. "I think he might. But we'd have to speak to Bishop Rowena first."

Nadia shrugged. "OK. Then we tell Ro to tell him. I reckon she'd be OK with it."

"So long as she doesn't tell anyone else," cautioned Tom. "Not until we say she can. You saw what the press were like outside the hospital. It's going to be ten times worse if they get the idea that we are talking about a parallel world with the Nazis in charge."

"Catastrophic," agreed Hen. "We tell her it's private for now and that she can only share it with her professor in New York."

"How're we going to do it?" wondered Alice. "If we ask her to join us, like now, my parents will want to know what we are talking about. They wouldn't want her being told something and them being left out. They're unhappy with us talking without them as it is. Like, they'll quiz her and she will have to refuse to tell them... or lie. Then they'll get annoyed. It'll be like... awful."

"Bishops can't lie," stated Nadia. "They ain't allowed to.

Remember the ninth commandment."

"One of us could get her on her own and tell her," suggested Alice. "What about you, Hen?"

"No, not me," he protested. "I reckon it should be Roxanne. Rox has more experience of the flipside than anyone. You'll tell her in just the right way, Rox. And you haven't got anyone who will want to quiz you about talking to her."

Tom agreed instantly. "Yes! Perfect. Rox's on her own, so is Rowena."

"Yeah. You do it," ordered Nadia.

Alice concurred. "Yes. Rox, you're the one." But Roxanne's eyes were glazed in thought.

"Rox?" called Hen. "Rox? You haven't said anything."

"Sorry, I was mentally on the flipside wondered what's happening there. OK. I'll talk to her."

"Great," whispered Alice. "And no one else has to say anything to anyone other than Ro or her professor until we all decide otherwise."

"Agreed," said Hen. "And that brings us on to the next thing we need to talk about. They haven't said what'll happen to us when we get back to Gatwick But I'm for insisting on going back to the Winterford. That way we won't be dragged apart as soon as we get to Britain. Debriefing or no debriefing.

Back to the Winterford. Back to base. And I can get my stuff and especially my phone."

"Yay," exalted Alice. "Phones! Back to, like, normal. I'd almost forgotten how to use one. I've become so used to living in a closed world where the only people you can talk to are those immediately around you. Like back in the stone age or something."

Tom laughed. He was delighted to see Alice brightening up. It was like the sun coming out from behind the clouds.

"And I think," put in Hen, "we should phone that youth worker to say thank you. We only met her once but she was on our case with Bishop Ro from the beginning, it seems."

Nadia felt obliged to put a dampener on the sunshine. "But let's not forget that monster Padget is still out there! We may not have heard the last of him. We need our phones so that we can warn each other if he turns up. Like, if I had my phone when I was collected from the youth club, I could'a told you what was up."

"You don't think he's going to be after our brains now, though, is he?" asked Alice.

"No. But you know what fascists are like," murmured Hen. "He's going to lay the blame for everything that's happened to his Daisychain organisation on us. He'll probably be bent on revenge."

Alice shivered. "You mean it may not be all over?"

"They haven't captured him yet, have they?" stated Roxanne. "Who knows what he's up to. After what has happened here, he's going to be livid! If I know anything about his type, he'll be after us for sure."

42

In Paris, Padget smiled to himself. The last he had heard was that the package had arrived. He had done his bit. Now all he had to do was lay low and, when the hue and cry had died down, return to the US. But he had to call his wife or she would not be happy - he did not want her raising concerns because she hadn't heard from him. He dialled her number and, when she didn't reply, left a voicemail message. It was fatal.

With nothing better to do, Padget mixed with his fellow tourists and made his way down the Champs-Elysées towards the Louvre - the palace at the centre of power in the days before the revolution at the end of the eighteenth century. Looking around, he reflected. *How many days in this current century before power in this city and all over the world will be ours?* If things went well, it could happen next spring - a new revolution that would not need a war; the world's armies would all come under Daisychain command. He saw himself being celebrated in this city - a hero of the movement. The code name "Daisychain" would then be confined to the history books - books that they would write.

It was as he crossed the Place de la Concorde that the

French police made their move. He did not have time to reflect that this was once the Place de la Révolution where many of the leading French aristocrats and others had met their deaths in the 1790s. Some instinct told him he was in danger. He looked up; he was being approached on three sides by policemen. He turned in the one direction there were none – south towards the bridge, but the police came together and followed him; he knew he was their target. He walked faster.

Crossing the bustling traffic on the square was no easy matter. He began to run; if only he could reach the bridge, he might be able to melt into the crowds of people and cars in the busy intersection of the Quai Anatole France and the Quai d'Orsay.

This could not be happening to him – he should not have run. He should have defied them, challenged them. After all, what did they have on him? But the sight of the men in blue panicked him. Truthfully, if he had been honest with himself, he knew it had all gone wrong the minute that damned professor had been outwitted by a bunch of pesky teenagers. He had feared it then.

But he might yet get away; amid screeching brakes and the sound of police whistles and sirens, he somehow managed to reach the Pont de la Concorde successfully. He had gained the middle of the bridge and the police were struggling against the traffic and the crowds. Just a few more paces; his lungs strained and his heart pounded... Just another fifty metres and he would be on the left bank and could melt into the crowds that thronged the Quai D'Orsay outside the Assemblée Nationale. But then, to his horror, he saw in front of him another group of men in uniform, calling on him to halt. He was trapped.

Donald Padget mounted the parapet and jumped.

The eye of a helmsman of a *bateau-mouche* passing beneath the bridge saw a man's body fall – a man in a casual but expensive-looking jacket and trousers, not your typical bridge jumper. He put the engines into reverse, pulling the boat up and he and the others who had seen the man fall stared at the place the jumper had entered the water. But neither the people aboard the boat nor the police and tourists peering down from above could see any sign of him.

43

Telling Bishop Rowena about the flipside didn't prove a problem. Roxanne asked if she could sit with her on the plane going home as she had no relative with her. That seemed a natural request. It worked out well because there was no one in the aisle seat and they had all the way to Gatwick to talk about it. Rowena listened both fascinated and horrified. These young people had been through far more extremes than anyone had guessed. There was no way Roxanne Battie was making this up, especially if it was confirmed by all five sensible bright young people.

Rowena agreed to take it straight to Professor Bradford. She promised she would tell no one else. She advised Roxanne and the others to say nothing to anyone for the time being. Roxanne assured her that that was exactly what they wanted and Rowena could rely on them not to utter a word until the right time came, if it ever did.

"It sounds like you made some good friends on your flipside," observed the bishop.

"Yeah. I was reconciled to staying there forever. I had a pretty rotten time of it here, anyway."

"But now?"

"One part of me is glad I'm back because that world is not a nice one outside the fellowship of the MPC, but I miss them, too. They've given me what I need to survive in this world without self harming, and that's something."

"And four friends for life," smiled the bishop.

"Yes. Nadia has adopted me as her sister."

"Perfect. Somehow I think you two will make a pretty big impact on this world."

Or even back there on the flipside, thought Roxanne to herself but she said nothing.

44

When they landed at Gatwick the group were met by officers of MI5 who ushered them past the clamouring press corps to a fleet of waiting cars to be taken to a local hotel.

The official questioning was eventually put a stop to by medical staff who said the young people needed to rest.

On the morning of the following day, a press conference was called and DI Renshaw and the five friends sat behind a desk. The factual questions were not difficult to answer. Alice found she could be truthful in everything she said if she simply left out the bits she didn't want to share. The hard questions were the personal ones about how you felt when someone kidnaps you. She heard herself answer by saying, "How would you feel if someone locked you inside a boat and you didn't know where you were going?" Then, amazingly, she surprised herself when she said, in answer to a question of what she would most like to do next. "Get back to school and study for my exams."

After the press conference, they learned that they would not be allowed back to the Winterford but they were delighted when all their things arrived in cardboard boxes – including their mobile phones! The following hours were taken up with charging them up and updating themselves.

Nadia and Roxanne went off and sat in a garden chatting by themselves as they explored their very limited numbers of contacts but Alice was into all the stuff from Beth and her other friends – some of it sent before she officially disappeared and quite a bit since, as Beth kept up her campaign to make sure she wasn't forgotten. When the news got out that she had been found in Norway, the numbers of texts and messages turned into hundreds. She never did get through it all. But the first thing she did was text Beth and then post a selfie with Tom on Instagram – which even got onto Yorkshire television.

That evening, Tom and Alice wandered alone into the shadows of the hotel garden and confirmed that their mutual attraction was not confined to the flipside. A kiss could be just as sweet under a tree in Sussex as in a theatre in Nazi Streatham.

Together they briefly ventured into the fifth. They didn't stay there long; they quickly re-emerged to resume their tender exchanges, glad to have gained control of their ability to flip; it had definitely become no longer an affliction but a gift.

On the third day at the Gatwick hotel, the authorities released the young people and their carers and with many tears they parted for their homes north, south and west.

There was to be no taking of buses or trains – they were transported home in official cars and seen safely into their houses before, at last, they were left to their own devices. Needless to say, the first thing they did was text the others to say they were home.

Fortunately, as they kept their heads down, new and more pressing things happened in the world and the reporters eventually disappeared. There was to be a brief resurgence of interest when Alice took part in and won a 400-metre race but there was no mention of anything to do with 5D and, of course, nothing was suspected of a parallel world.

45

Roxanne joined Nadia in her secondary school. They were put back into year ten. They didn't argue - they knew how far away they were from doing all they were capable of and that, especially in Roxanne's case, they had been under-performing for years. Nadia was especially happy to learn that Demon Dean Sharman had already left school and was labouring on a building site. She was reliably informed that he had grown up overnight and was happy doing what he was. She didn't strive hard to discover his whereabouts, though.

On a couple of occasions in the next few months, Hen had travelled to Bristol by train and spent a weekend with the girls. He said it was a breath of fresh air from his studies in Wincanton college. Now he had mastered the art of curtailing his flipping, things were back to almost normal - his father still wanted him to go into engineering but Hen was holding out for pure maths.

Alice spent most of the school holidays in West Bay. Her parents knew when they were defeated and quickly came to like Tom. What was there not to like about him - even if he was never going to become a millionaire, a lawyer or a famous surgeon?

The first time they were all united was when Bishop Rowena came to London with Professor Bradford. This was on the eve of Professor William's trial in the Old Bailey and Bishop Rowena, each of the young people and some of their parents had been called as witnesses.

Testifying at Prof W's trial proved scary enough – even for Nadia – to ensure they did not feel like flipping. All five, plus others from the Winterford Clinic, tried to answer the barristers' questions as clearly and honestly as they could, but it didn't stop them feeling stupid at times. They were asked why they had only come to believe late on that their professor was prepared to kill – why had not they been suspicious from the beginning? Was it that they were too naïve as to think he wouldn't consider murder?

But the fact is: it is always easier to see things more clearly after the event when all the little clues add up. At the time, in the culture that Prof W promoted inside the clinic, it was difficult to see through his charm. He was, after all, genuine in wanting to get to understand the phenomenon. He had told his subjects they were sick and he was looking for a cure. Ninety-five per cent of the time his ambitions coincided with keeping his patients safe and in good health.

Alice testified that, in her opinion, in the beginning, he had not been considering any of them as subjects for dissection - he had been frustrated but he was prepared to wait. It was only when Donald Padget put pressure on him for results that he came to contemplate a short cut.

"We know he was threatened," she explained. "Hen - erm, Christopher - said he had overheard an argument. Mr Padget told the professor that he had only a few months before Mr Padget pulled the plug."

"You mean," interrupted the barrister to clarify the point, "call in his debts."

"Yes. Our plan was to use those months to try and find out more about the fifth ourselves. There didn't seem any point in going home at that stage - we had already put off sitting our GCSEs and we still hadn't learned how to control our flips. I think, maybe, Professor Williams believed Mr Padget was only lending him the money to help - a kind of investment. It was only later that we found out just how good he and his cronies were at making lies sound like the truth. But then, in June, Mr Padget turned nasty and Professor Williams gave in to him."

"So," continued the barrister, "eventually, when you were in Norway, the opportunity arose for the professor to conduct his experiments. How did he behave towards you, then?"

"I don't think he ever really wanted to kill us... left to

himself. I reckon he was, sort of, on our side, especially after we rescued him on the island."

The defence put their client on the stand. He had pleaded guilty to complicity with a terrorist organisation but not guilty of plotting to kill any of his subjects. He said that he had been the victim of intimidation; he did not support the aims of the terrorists. As he was cross-examined by the prosecution, he showed genuine remorse.

One mitigating fact, his lawyer explained, was the role he had played in ensuring that a vital incriminating document had survived the devastating fire in the warehouse – a file that had contained the names and contact details of many of the key Daisychain players around the world. It had led to mass arrests and to the virtual dissolution of the Daisychain organisation.

The prosecution pointed out, however, that this had only been achieved by pure chance, as the defendant had merely used it to splint a man's arm. But in his summing up, the defence attorney highlighted the fact that his client had had no need to risk his life saving another man – a Norwegian soldier who would be forever grateful to him – and who had appeared as a character witness. And if his client had been truly on the side of the terrorists, he would have taken special care not to have allowed the document to survive. While the defence did not mean to suggest that the professor's *intention* had been, at that moment, to hand over a vital document, he was, nevertheless, glad that he had. The word Prof W used was "serendipitous".

In committing Professor Williams to prison, the judge said the director of the Winterford had not only plotted murder but had consistently lied to his colleagues, misled his peers and, above all, betrayed the trust of his charges. These were mostly young people, half under the age of eighteen, and included five fifteen-year-old residents whose parents and guardians had entrusted them to Professor Williams in order to research into a cure for a condition that was on the edges of medical science. Their willingness to trust Williams could have proved fatal and would have done if it had not been for the five astute young people. The bravery of these young people and their devotion to each other, was to be commended. It was not through the professor's actions that the terrorists had been foiled, but the resistance of five determined and remarkable teenagers.

However, the judge explained that Professor Williams had registered a guilty plea and shown remorse. The judge did not see him as an evil man but one with a single-minded ambition combined with a scientific research project that had led him into dangerous waters, far deeper than he could cope with. He sentenced him to eight years.

The judge recommended that, in future, teenagers who had had no history of over-playing a situation should be listened to – even if it involved a complaint against a well-respected member of society. He concluded that, on the whole, society does not listen enough to its young people – this should be something that society might be willing to change.

46

After Prof W had been driven away, the press were kept at bay at the front of the courthouse. The police made a statement on their behalf as Nadia, Tom, Hen, Roxanne and Alice were ushered with their families and guardians through the rear entrance. But some enterprising photographers had covered that way, too.

"Excuse us," announced Hen. "We'll see you later."

The five held hands and, there and then, flipped into the fifth just long and far enough to disappear and avoid the scrum.

A few moments later they landed gently at the feet of Prof Bradford and Bishop Rowena who stood together several hundred metres from the gaggle of reporters still wondering where the five had gone.

"That was neatly done!" exclaimed Bradford. "I see you're quite the experts. You seem to be getting a good control of your gift. Where do you want to take it from here?"

They looked at each other. "Together," said Alice. "We have to find a way of staying together." There was no way they felt they could live forever back among people in the communities from which they had come - people who did not begin to understand what they had been through and what being able to access new dimensions meant. They were on a life journey, and above all, they needed to be together - they belonged together like brothers and sisters.

Roxanne, who up until this time had not said much, felt this was probably the time to speak. "Over there, on the flipside, things are bad. We shouldn't just go on as if there ain't another world - like, ignore it."

Professor Bradford grew animated. "Yes. I meant to ask you about that. You've not said much about that world since you got back from Norway. Rowena explained I was allowed to be let into the secret."

Hen glanced at his fellow 5D travellers. "I guess we didn't want to sound... How shall I put it?"

"Nuts!" supplied Nadia.

"Well put," laughed Hen.

"But we ain't," said Nadia with feeling, adding, "Roxanne, you're gonna go back, ain't you? It's obvious, innit? Here, you ain't got no family. Until you met us, you hadn't got anyone to call your own. Life was real hard for you but over there you found people who cared, you fitted in. You even had this boy who—"

"That weren't ever going anywhere," stated Roxanne,

crisply.

"Nah. But you were *wanted*," affirmed Nadia. "You had a part to play in that world, Rox."

"You're right. And I think about them all, all the time."

"But Roxanne you *do* belong here," put in Alice, "I mean you were born on this side, and you'll always have *us*. 'All for one' remember."

"And you can stay with me, Rox," confirmed Nadia, "as long as you like. Bristol ain't that great for some but, if you meet the right people, it has its good side."

"Maybe," shrugged Roxanne. "Perhaps I'll make it my home – I like it. I'll finish my GCSEs but then – who knows."

"Well, Roxanne, you seem to have your immediate future worked out," said Prof Bradford, smiling.

Then, striking a serious note, he added, "I have a proposal for you all. I think you should, now, finish your studies, your vocational qualifications or whatever you have planned. But then, when you are eighteen, I would like you to come to New York and help my research. What do you say? Would you like to come to New York and be part of my team? At my expense, of course."

"New York?!" exclaimed Alice.

"I'm afraid so. But we are fairly relaxed. You could come back to Britain whenever you need. Be at home for your birthdays, Christmas and Thanksgiving..."

"Well, then. Yeah. If you think..." said Tom, still wondering whether this was a dream. "New York!"

"Yay, New York!" exclaimed Alice, again. "Hey Hen, you are up for this aren't you... when you're eighteen?"

"Certainly. If I can contribute in any way to the further understanding of the phenomena that—"

"Me? Me, too?" marvelled Nadia. "But I'm not very clever like Hen."

"Nadia," said the professor in a sincere tone, "you can leave the science to the scientists. The boy or girl that flips for the first time is going to be really scared, and I believe you are going to be able to help them more than anyone because you know exactly how they are feeling. You can say it as it is, and you don't complicate it with all the words I tend to use."

Hen smiled. "Nadia is so cool - she just has to be part of anything we do. And Rox. We stick together!"

"All for one—" began Nadia.

"And one for all," they chorused.

"By the time you're eighteen, Rox, the revolution might be over," suggested Nadia, squeezing her friend, "then you could come to New York, too."

"It's a deal, then?" asked Prof Bradford.

Alice looked at the others and smiled. "Deal?"

Prof Bradford held up his hand in a high-five. Nadia met it with force.

"Course," she confirmed. "Ace."

"Roxanne?" asked the professor.

"Sure. If I'm not on the flipside."

The parents and relatives eventually found their daughters and sons. They weren't so sure about going to America.

Alice's dad reminded everyone the Donald Padget was an American and he had still not been found. What if he wanted to get back at the young people?

"Ro and I will look after them. We promise," undertook Professor Bradford.

"Ro? We?" queried Nadia.

"I m... mean Bishop Rowena," stammered Bradford, giving Rowena a sideways glance.

Nadia laughed. "'Ro'! 'We'! You're an item, ain't you?"

"That is one way of putting it, Nadia," admitted Rowena. "It was through you that we met... But it isn't official, so we'd be grateful if you didn't say anything just yet."

"That depends," said Hen with a delighted but mock-wicked grin, "on how much you are willing to pay us for introduction fees."

"Yeah," joked Alice. "We'll be setting ourselves up as the Fifth Dimension Marriage Agency: all profits to 5D research."

Professor Bradford smiled. "Sounds good to me. Except I haven't actually proposed yet."

"I reckon you're made for each other," affirmed Tom. "Imagine, married to a bishop!"

The professor laughed. "I know. Scary, isn't it? But I reckon I'll survive... If she'll have me."

"Who says I want to be married to a scientist?" responded Rowena, playfully.

"What do you get when you cross a scientist with a bishop?" asked Nadia.

"I couldn't begin to guess," said Rowena. "But I think I'm a bit long in the tooth to have babies."

"You don't have babies," explained Nadia. "You get five 5D young adults!... Go on, Ro, say yes!"

"Well, all right. Yes, I will. I will marry you Red, if it means I get to see these young people again."

"Course!" declared Nadia. "That's the deal and me, Rox and Alice can be bridesmaids... So long as it ain't pink."

"Go on! You may kiss the bride," urged Alice.

"Right," muttered Bradford, blushing and changing the subject. "Back to the subject of 5D research. That's all settled then. When you're eighteen—"

"Kiss the bride," interrupted Alice, insistently.

Bishop Rowena proffered her cheek and Prof Bradford kissed it.

"Now, that will have to do," Rowena said firmly, as Alice opened her mouth to speak again.

"New York is a long way from Britain for our girl," put in Alice's father, changing the tone and becoming serious. "She will still be very young even when she has turned eighteen. Eighteen is nothing."

Alice pleaded. "Dad. Eighteen is *adult*. Grown up!"

Alice's mum came to her rescue. "She's been through far more than we ever have and survived. I reckon New York'll be a doddle for her. Let's face it, we no longer have a child, darling, our daughter is fast becoming a young woman."

"It may be all right for her, but it won't be so easy for us," mumbled her dad.

"No. But it's the price parents have to pay to have someone special – and we wouldn't want it any other way, would we?"

"Special? She is that!" confirmed her father kissing his daughter. "Darling, if you want to go, then it seems we're not going to stop you."

"Let's get out of here," declared Alice, feeling embarrassed and tugging at Tom's hand.

"Altogether then!" exclaimed Tom. "Coming Nadia?"

"You bet!"

The press had eventually spotted them and the advancing pack pounced but not before the excitement raised the adrenaline of the five friends. Prof Bradford walked forward to address the reporters, taking the attention of the cameras, as Alice reached out to Nadia and Rox and all five let themselves go into the flip.

"A month ago I thought my daughter was a sick little girl," murmured Nadia's dad quietly to the other parents. "Now I can see her for what she really is - a gifted young woman... Fancy going for a drink?"

It was while they relaxed inside the Magpie and Stump that the parents and relatives of four 5D teenage flippers founded the Fifth Dimension Support Group for parents and relatives.

Later, in a Subway, Rowena treated the youngsters to subs and coke.

"Where do you reckon Padget's got to?" wondered Nadia.

"No idea," said Hen. "If I didn't know better I would say he's flipped."

"Nah, he never did that," objected Alice. "He couldn't have done... could he?"

"If he's on the flipside, Rox'll be on to him!" spat Nadia.

"In case you come across him and you want my help," joked Rowena, "what's the password going to be? I'm afraid I had to reveal 'cheesy chips' in the trial. What else don't you like Hen?"

"Luke-warm, sticky rice pudding with jam in it," replied Hen.

Rowena laughed. "That's a long password but it'll do. Let's hope you never need it! Anyway, we must stay in touch, whatever. Don't forget to keep me posted on your progress."

"Course!" promised Nadia.

Thank you for reading the Flip trilogy.

1. *Flip! On the Edge*
2. *Beyond the Horizon*
3. *The Daisychain.*

If you have enjoyed this book, please
recommend it to your friends
and rate it on Goodreads:
https://www.goodreads.com

and on Amazon:
https://www.amazon.co.uk/s?k=trevor+stubbs

If you can write a short review, too,
that would be brilliant.

Trevor Stubbs
www.trevorstubbs.co.uk

ACKNOWLEDGEMENTS

Writing a story involves teamwork. Although the idea, the plot and the characters of *Flip* have all been mine, I am grateful to some lovely people who have invested time and patience in reading the various drafts.

I would like to thank Laurie Thorpe, Sarah Voss and Jo Ullah, artist and author (https://www.joullah.com) for their advice and patience. Jo, in particular, has worked hard at reading several drafts; I am enormously indebted to her.

As always, my work would never have come about if it were not for the huge commitment, encouragement, editing and sound advice of my wife, Tina.

I also want to thank the members of the Bristol branch of the Alliance of Independent Authors and the Association of Christian Writers for all that I have learnt and continue to learn from them.

Finally, I thank the amazing young people I meet as a youth volunteer. They never cease to inspire me.

I give all the proceeds of my books over and above the cost of printing to charity. My default charity is Confident Children out of Conflict (http://confidentchildren.org) in Juba, South Sudan, so I thank you for your purchase.

I hope you have enjoyed reading the *Flip!* trilogy.

Trevor Stubbs

The White Gates Adventures

by Trevor Stubbs

The Kicking Tree

Ultimate Justice

Winds & Wonders

The Spark

Meet Jack Smith (18) from Planet Earth - angry and drifting - and Jalli Rarga (17) from Planet Raika in the Andromeda Galaxy, struggling to be different from other girls.

Step with them through strange white gates into wonderful new worlds.

Adventure - Sci-Fi - Fear - Fun - Humour - Love

Explore outwards into the vast universe and inwards to the human heart where everyone matters.

From *The Kicking Tree* by Trevor Stubbs

Beyond the white gate, Jalli could no longer hear the sound of the traffic behind her; all she was aware of was birdsong and a gentle buzzing that she associated with parmandas – the life-cycle of which she was now an expert, or so Mr Bandi had said. Everything about Wanulka seemed to have vanished. She appeared to be in an entirely new world.

The very quality of the air was different – it was softer and sweeter than anything she had experienced anywhere. Even the green-grassed borders beneath the trees beside Wanulka beach – grass which the city council kept constantly watered – felt very coarse compared with the carpet of lawn on which she now stood.

It was a wonderful experience. She debated if she had "passed over" somehow, as Grandma might say. This was exactly like the place she expected heaven to be – so different and so beautiful.

She couldn't see anyone else there, but she felt an overwhelming sense of welcome. Strangely, she did not in the least feel like an intruder. In some miraculous way, it was "hers" to enjoy. Why? She had only just stepped onto the lawn and now she was feeling like she had belonged here forever. Had she experienced something like this as a child perhaps? Was she in some kind of dream?

REVIEWS FOR THE KICKING TREE

"I think this book is amazing. I like the fact that almost nothing bad happens, but that you still want to read more. It is hard to put away and there is not a sentence in the book that is boring."

Ebba (Goodreads)

"This book is one of the most special books I've ever read. In a good way. It's a love story. But it's not really a love story - it's about two people falling love. It's an SF book. But it's not really an SF book: there is some time (perhaps wormhole?) travelling going on and there are spaceships. It's also a fantasy story. But it's not really a fantasy story..."

Lynn (Goodreads)

"Wonderful story. It's a great adventure that made me cry. I love the two main characters who meet across the universe..."

Miss S (Amazon)

"... a perfect book for the adult-literacy teacher trying to encourage teens to read, with it's strong narrative structure, simple vocabulary and positive, active role models. There are all too few authors who write well for this market, and Stubbs is one of them."

Church Times

"Trevor Stubbs has an interesting philosophy of life: 'I hate injustice and oppression, especially against the weak and the vulnerable and want to speak out.' Trevor uses his undoubted skills as a master storyteller and a magical weaver of tales to bring about such justice."

That's Book and Entertainment